ZERO DARK THIRTY

ZERO DARK THIRTY

SCREENPLAY BY MARK BOAL

INTRODUCTION BY KATHRYN BIGELOW

newmarket press
for itbooks
AN IMPRINT OF HARPERCOLLINS*PUBLISHERS*

A Newmarket Shooting Script® Series Book

HarperCollins books may be purchased for educational, business, or sales promotional use. For infor-mation please e-mail the Special Markets Department at SPsales@harpercollins.com.

First Newmarket press for It Books edition published 2013.

Library of Congress Cataloging-in-Publication Data is available upon request.

ISBN 978-0-06-227634-6

13 14 15 16 17 10 9 8 7 6 5 4 3 2

CONTENTS

INTRODUCTION

BY KATHRYN BIGELOW

After our successful collaboration on *The Hurt Locker*, Mark Boal pitched me a film about the decade-long and, at the time, inconclusive hunt for the world's most dangerous man, Osama bin Laden. In the middle of this process, history was made in that now legendary raid, and we were faced with having either to abandon the project or to pivot in a new direction. Not one to quit anything, Mark forged ahead with renewed purpose and trotted the globe in search of answers to our questions about the hunt, that raid, and the people behind it that had never been addressed in any comprehensive manner.

His research turned up incredible discoveries about the anonymous operatives who work behind the scenes. Along the way he recognized there was more to their story than anyone knew, and our excitement about the project escalated as we secured independent financing from Annapurna and distribution agreements with Sony Pictures and Universal Pictures International.

Still, I was not prepared for the impact his ultimate screenplay would have on me. He approached the topic, the hunt, the real world inhabitants of this account in an entirely innovative way, as if he was creating a new genre, one that tells a truthful story in searing scenes, based on bona fide reporting, but that is dramatized, as motion pictures necessarily are, in its specific dialogue and unknowable, intimate moments.

What appealed to me as a director was its sense of urgency, its immediacy, both fresh and raw; moreover, that its story presented a living history, one that was unfolding before the world in real time. At the same time, as the thriller aspects of the story unfolded, the material also raised deep moral questions about the lines that were crossed in the war on terror, and the nature of courage and persistence in a world where the normal rules don't seem to apply.

The script also immersed me in a way I did not anticipate; its finely drawn characters, the intricate and snappy dialogue, gripping action, and truly human moments drew me in instantly. As for his portrayal of the central character, Maya, he has to my mind presented a unique female heroine unfettered by clichés, allowing us to experience this epic story through a lens that is both intimate and, at the end of the day, totally human.

On a broader level, I felt that with this screenplay we could perhaps spark a conversation about the shadowy lives of those in the intelligence community, the price they've paid for their work, and the murky deeds that were done over this dark decade in the name of national security. That feels to me like a film worth making and a conversation worth having, now more than ever.

ZERO DARK THIRTY

by Mark Boal

FROM BLACK, VOICES EMERGE--

We hear the actual recorded emergency calls made by World
Trade Center office workers to police and fire departments
after the planes struck on 9/11, just before the buildings
collapsed.

TITLE OVER: SEPTEMBER 11, 2001

We listen to fragments from a number of these calls...starting
with pleas for help, building to a panic, ending with the
caller's grim acceptance that help will not arrive, that the
situation is hopeless, that they are about to die.

                                                    CUT TO:

TITLE OVER: TWO YEARS LATER

INT. BLACK SITE - INTERROGATION ROOM

                    DANIEL
          I own you, Ammar. You belong to me.
          Look at me.

This is DANIEL STANTON, the CIA's man in Islamabad - a big
American, late 30's, with a long, anarchical beard snaking
down to his tattooed neck. He looks like a paramilitary
hipster, a punk rocker with a Glock.

                    DANIEL (CONT'D)
               (explaining the rules)
          If you don't look at me when I talk
          to you. I hurt you. If you step off
          this mat, I hurt you. If you lie to
          me, I'm gonna hurt you. Now, Look
          at me.

His prisoner, AMMAR, stands on a decaying gym mat, surrounded
by four GUARDS whose faces are covered in ski masks.

Ammar looks down. Instantly: the guards rush Ammar, punching
and kicking.

                    DANIEL (CONT'D)
          Look at me, Ammar.

Notably, one of the GUARDS wearing a ski mask does not take
part in the beating.

EXT. BLACK SITE - LATER

Daniel and the masked figures emerge from the interrogation
room into the light of day. They remove their masks and we
see that one is a beautiful young woman in her mid-twenties.

She has a pale, milky innocence and bright blue eyes, thin
and somewhat frail looking, yet possessing a steely core

that we will come to realize is off-the-charts. This is
MAYA, a CIA targeter and subject-matter expert on her first
overseas assignment.

> DANIEL
> (to the guard)
> Are we gonna board up these windows
> or what?
> (to Maya)
> Just off the plane from Washington,
> you're rocking your best suit for
> your first interrogation, and then
> you get this guy. It's not always
> this intense.

> MAYA
> I'm fine.

She's not.

> DANIEL
> Just so you know, it's going to take
> awhile. He has to learn how helpless
> he is. Let's get a coffee.

> MAYA
> No, we should go back in.

Something about the strange intensity of her expression makes
Daniel reconsider and he turns back to the interrogation
room.

> DANIEL
> You know, there's no shame if you
> wanna watch from the monitor.

She shakes her head.

> DANIEL (CONT'D)
> Alright.

At the door, Daniel hands the ski mask back to Maya.

> DANIEL (CONT'D)
> You might want to put this on.

> MAYA
> You're not wearing one. Is he ever
> getting out?

> DANIEL
> Never.

CUT TO:

INT. INTERROGATION ROOM - LATER

SUPERIMPOSE: CIA BLACK SITE - UNDISCLOSED LOCATION

Ammar, bruised from the beating, is restrained with ropes.

Maya stands a few feet behind Daniel, attentive, wary of what is to come. This is her first interrogation and she is on the verge of vomiting from the stench in the room. She looks around at the sound-proofed walls, the puddles of water on the floor.

>   DANIEL
>   Right now, this is about you coming
>   to terms with your situation. It's
>   you and me, bro. I want you to
>   understand that I know you, that
>   I've been studying you for a very
>   long time. I could have had you
>   killed Karachi. But I let you live
>   so you and I could talk.

>   AMMAR
>   (resistant)
>   You beat me when my hands are tied.
>   I won't talk to you.

>   DANIEL
>   Life isn't always fair, my friend.
>   Did you really think that when we
>   got you, I'd be a nice fucking guy?

>   AMMAR
>   You're a mid-level guy. You're a
>   garbage man in a corporation. Why
>   should I respect you?

>   DANIEL
>   And you're a money man. A paperboy!

Daniel paces around Ammar, anger rising.

>   DANIEL (CONT'D)
>   A disgrace to humanity! You and
>   your uncle murdered three thousand
>   innocent people. I have your name
>   on a five-thousand dollar transfer
>   via Western Union to a 9/11 hijacker.

He leans into Ammar's ear. Uncomfortably close.

>   DANIEL (CONT'D)
>   And you got popped with 150 kilograms
>   of high explosives in your house!
>   AND THEN YOU DARE QUESTION ME?!

And then Daniel smiles, laughs. Mercurial.

>   DANIEL (CONT'D)
>   I'm just fucking with you.

Beat. He laughs again.

                    DANIEL (CONT'D)
          I don't want to talk about 9/11.
          What I want to focus on is the Saudi
          group.

Daniel shows him a photo.

                    DANIEL (CONT'D)
          That there is Hazem al-Kashmiri.
          And I know this dude is up to some
          serious shit, and what I want from
          you is his Saudi email.
                    (pause)
          Feel free to jump in.
                    (pause)
          Ammar, bro, I know that you know
          this dude, just give me his
          email...and I will give you a blanket.
          I will give you a blanket and some
          solid food.

No response from Ammar. Daniel starts putting on his gloves.

                    DANIEL (CONT'D)
          I know that you know him.

                    AMMAR
          I told you before, I won't talk to
          you.

                    DANIEL
          Have it your way.
                    (to the masks)
          Let's go.

It all happens in a flash: in one swift motion, Daniel pushes
Ammar to the floor, the guards pin his limbs, and Daniel
smothers Ammar's face with a towel.

Ammar thrashes. Daniel considers his next move.

                    DANIEL (CONT'D)
                    (to Maya)
          Grab the bucket.

Maya follows Daniel's gesture to the corner of the room,
where there's an ICE CHEST filled with WATER and a PLASTIC
PITCHER.

                    DANIEL (CONT'D)
          Put some water in it.

She dips the pitcher in the water, hands shaking.

                    DANIEL (CONT'D)
          C'mon, let's go.

The stress and strain on her face is enormous as she brings
the bucket back to Daniel.

Daniel starts pouring the water on Ammar's face, which is now covered by a towel. Ammar thrashes with rising panic.

                    DANIEL (CONT'D)
          Hazem was a friend of Ramzi Yousef,
          you guys met in Tunisia back in the
          70s.

                    AMMAR
               (gasping for breath)
          I don't know, you asshole.

Maya shakes her head "no."

                    MAYA
          That's not credible.

                    AMMAR
               (screaming)
          Why are you doing this to me?

                    DANIEL
          You're a terrorist, that's why I'm
          doing it to you.

                    AMMAR
          Fuck you.

Daniel pours water over the towel so it hits Ammar's nose.

                    DANIEL
          I want emails of the rest of the
          Saudi group. Give me emails of the
          rest of the Saudi group! Give me
          one email, and I will stop this!

Ammar doesn't speak. He can't.

                    DANIEL (CONT'D)
          Who's in the Saudi group, and what's
          the target? Where was the last time
          you saw bin Laden? WHERE WAS THE
          LAST TIME YOU SAW BIN LADEN?

Daniel throws the pitcher, rips the rag off Ammar's mouth: and water spurts out - Ammar nearly drowned. He gasps for air.

                    DANIEL (CONT'D)
          This is what defeat looks like, bro.
          Your jihad is over.

Daniel stands.

                    DANIEL (CONT'D)
          Get him up.

The guards bring Ammar to his feet.

Daniel, shifting his persona yet again, touches Ammar's face and speaks to him with the comforting tenor of a therapist.

> DANIEL (CONT'D)
> Try to understand the concept here.
> I have time, you don't. I have other
> things to do, you don't.
> (beat)
> It's cool that you're strong. I
> respect it, I do. But in the end,
> everybody breaks, bro. It's biology.

Dan and Maya exit.

They've learned nothing.

                                        CUT TO:

EXT. ISLAMABAD, PAKISTAN - MORNING

SUPERIMPOSE: ISLAMABAD, PAKISTAN

A colorful, dusty city. Busy markets. Poor children. Dense traffic.

Meanwhile, across town:

EXT. DIPLOMATIC QUARTER - ISLAMABAD - DAY

National flags. Imposing buildings. Armed guards. The outpost of a superpower.

Maya drives through the checkpoint and up to the main gate.

SUPERIMPOSE: UNITED STATES EMBASSY, ISLAMABAD

                                        CUT TO:

INT. AMERICAN EMBASSY CIA SECTION - STAIRCASE - ISLAMABAD

Descending the lobby staircase with Daniel is JOSEPH BRADLEY, Chief of Station, Pakistan, a smooth, vain, sophisticated former case officer who hasn't quite buffed all the blood out of his fingernails.

> BRADLEY
> How did it go the other night?

> DANIEL
> It was good. The local cops need
> tactical help. But he's Tier fucking
> One, baby. There's your money maker.

> BRADLEY
> This is the guy that's KSM's nephew?
> What's his issue?

> DANIEL
> He's being a dick.

> BRADLEY
> If he's trying to outsmart you, tell
> him about your PhD.

> DANIEL
> I am going to have to turn up the
> heat. He needs to give us the Saudi
> group *now*.

They reach the lobby, where they can see Maya sitting in the
holding area. They walk towards her as Bradley considers
what Daniel is asking for.

INT. AMERICAN EMBASSY CIA SECTION - STAIRCASE/LOBBY

> BRADLEY
> He's gotta have that - given the
> family ties.

Permission granted, Daniel reassures his boss.

> DANIEL
> Tight with his uncle, prints all
> over the 9/11 money.

Daniel knocks on the glass for Maya to come in.

> DANIEL (CONT'D)
> (to Bradley, clocking
> her good looks)
> Was I lying or what?

The guard opens the door and Maya comes through - not many
females come through that door.

> DANIEL (CONT'D)
> (to Maya)
> Maya, this is Joseph Bradley, our
> illustrious station chief.
> (as they shake hands)
> Joe and I did Iraq together.

> BRADLEY
> And we continue our Christian mission
> here. Nice to meet you.

> MAYA
> You too, Sir.

> BRADLEY
> How was your flight?

They walk down the lobby towards the Secure Wing.

> MAYA
> Fine.

                    DANIEL
          She's been having a great time ever
          since she got in, isn't that right?

                    BRADLEY
          How do you like Pakistan so far?

                    MAYA
          It's kinda fucked up.

                    BRADLEY
          You volunteered for this didn't you?

                    MAYA
     No.

Bradley smiles. He knew she didn't volunteer.

They reach a secure area and Bradley checks Maya through an
electronic door.

                    BRADLEY
               (to Maya)
          Third floor, northeast corner.

She goes through and Daniel and Bradley watch her walk away.

                    DANIEL
          Don't you think she's a little young
          for the hard stuff?

                    BRADLEY
          Washington says she's a killer.

                    DANIEL
          The children's crusade.

                    BRADLEY
          They want the next generation on the
          field. Listen, I have a meeting
          with ISI in twenty minutes.

                    DANIEL
          They're slow rolling us in Lahore -
          you might want to bitch about that.

                    BRADLEY
          Did you see the cable from London?

                    DANIEL
          Dude, I've been in a dark room with
          another man for the last two days.

                                        CUT TO:

INT. AMERICAN EMBASSY CIA SECTION - MAYA'S CUBICLE

Maya finds her desk. It's covered with grime. She tries to clean it as best she can, then sits and looks at the blank log-in screen of her computer.

INT. AMERICAN EMBASSY CIA SECTION - CONFERENCE ROOM

A group of thirty-somethings filing in for a meeting, chatting, comradery, taking seats around a conference table.

We will get to know:

JACK, mid-40s, a scruffy teddy bear, the liaison from the National Security Agency (NSA).

JESSICA, 30s, an experienced targeter, and the only woman in the station who wears a skirt.

> JACK
> Some dude tells the Malaysian station that his nephew works with a guy who knows a guy--

> JESSICA
> Here we go.

> JACK
> Hold on - He goes to a big feast in Bangkok about a year ago. The guest of honor? Usama bin Laden.

Laughter in the room.

> JACK (CONT'D)
> So I say, was Tupac there too?

> JESSICA
> Right, but you forgot - you forgot Mullah Omar.

J.J. and JEREMY, two case officers, continue the banter:

> JEREMY
> (sarcastically)
> This is worth 5 million bucks.

> J.J.
> You know we're going to have to chase it down.

> JEREMY
> That's me, man. No job too small.

> JACK
> That's why I have a gift for you, my friend.

Jack hands Jeremy a piece of paper. Daniel and Maya enter, a little late.

                    DANIEL
          Everyone, this is Maya. Maya,
          everyone. Please don't ask how it's
          going with Ammar because she's not
          going to fucking tell you.

                    JESSICA
          Ammar is withholding?

Daniel nods.

                    JESSICA (CONT'D)
               (reading from her
                file)
          Washington assesses that Abu Faraj
          is officially our new number three -

JESSICA moves to a wall chart of AQ leadership and repositions Abu Faraj's mugshot to number three in the line, two down from Usama bin Laden. Meanwhile, in the background, the riffs continue -

                    DANIEL
          - Best man for it.

                    JACK (O.S.)
          London station is already asking if
          we think he's in contact with anyone
          in the U.K.

                    JEREMY
          Like we're just keeping it from them.

Jessica sits back down and gets down to business.

                    JESSICA
          The Jordanians are being really
          helpful with Ammar's transit papers.

Jessica passes Daniel a file.

                    DANIEL
          Any imminent threats in here?

                    JESSICA
          They want the Consulate, the Marriott,
          it's low security. And they've got
          Majid Kahn talking about gas stations
          in the US.

                    DANIEL
          And that's a conversation?

Jessica shrugs. At this point, she believes that it is merely a conversation - not a fully realized plot.

                         JESSICA
          Honestly? There are six hundred
          questions in there. I'd concentrate
          on Heathrow. The Saudis. Does it
          matter what Faraj thinks about
          Heathrow? How much latitude does he
          get to pick targets?

                         DANIEL
          I think he'll give up the Saudis.
          But Heathrow is gonna be tough.
          Anyway. Anything from last night?

                         J.J.
          Quetta base thinks they have a bead
          on the Arabs that escaped, and they're
          going to meet with the ISI this
          afternoon, hopefully to set up a
          raid down there.

                         DANIEL
          Great.

                         JEREMY
          And Lahore reporting ISI down there
          was painfully slow last night. Again.
          I'm beginning to think it's not
          incompetence.

                         DANIEL
          I agree, I spoke to the Chief about
          that. Anything on bin Laden?

                         JESSICA
               (reading from a cable)
          A farmer on the Afghan border near
          Tora Bora reports: a diamond shaped
          pattern in the hills, tall male in
          the center of the diamond, flanked
          by four guards. It's consistent
          with UBL's movements.

                         JEREMY
          That's supposed to be his royal guard?

                         MAYA
          That's pre-9/11 behavior.

Jessica doesn't appreciate the challenge.

                         JESSICA
               (chilly)
          We don't have reason to believe he's
          changed security tactics.

                         MAYA
          We invaded Afghanistan. That's a
          reason.

And so the rivalry begins.

>   J.J.
>   Hey, boss, I got a guy for five
>   thousand bucks, he can set up a taxi
>   stand and snoop around a bit.

>   DANIEL
>   No, don't need him, the diamond
>   sighting is bullshit. See if the
>   Paks will send someone to talk to
>   the farmer. Anything else? We need
>   to be putting runs on the board
>   against Faraj. Speak to the case
>   officers who didn't see fit to make
>   it today. And thank them.

INT. MAYA'S APARTMENT - ISLAMABAD

The loud WAILING of the early morning call to prayer from
the loudspeakers of a nearby mosque wakes Maya on the couch.

>   CUT TO:

INT. BLACK SITE - AFTERNOON

Daniel and the guards enter Ammar's cell with Maya. Daniel
switches on a floodlight, awakening Ammar.

>   DANIEL
>   Let's take it easy today, huh?

Daniel hands Ammar a bottle of orange juice and a bag of
falafel.

>   DANIEL (CONT'D)
>   Hungry? The food in here sucks so I
>   got you some of this.

Ammar grabs the lunch sack and scarfs down the falafels.

>   DANIEL (CONT'D)
>   Richard Reid, wow. I was thinking
>   about him. The guy gets a bomb in
>   his shoe on a plane. Unbelievable.
>   You know him, don't you?

Slowly, Ammar nods.

>   AMMAR
>   Yes.

>   DANIEL
>   I'm glad you said that. I have an
>   email from you to him. I've had all
>   your coms for years, bro. Who else
>   is in your Saudi group?

                    AMMAR
          I just handed out some cash for them.
          I didn't know who the guys were.

                    DANIEL
          When you lie to me, I hurt you.

                    AMMAR
          Please.

                    DANIEL
          I believe you. I do, I believe you.

Beat.

                    DANIEL (CONT'D)
          Do you want the water again, or do
          you want something else?

                    AMMAR
          Please.

                    DANIEL
          Just give me a name.

                    AMMAR
          I don't--

Daniel jumps up.

                    AMMAR (CONT'D)
          I don't know.

Daniel kicks out the chair from under Ammar. The masked
guards walk to the rope pulleys.

                    DANIEL
          You see how this works? You don't
          mind if my female colleague sees
          your junk, do you?

Daniel pulls down Ammar's pants. Maya flinches at the bare
nakedness.

                    DANIEL (CONT'D)
          Dude, you shit your pants.

Daniel turns to Maya -

                    DANIEL (CONT'D)
          You stay here, I'll be back.

Daniel goes out, leaving Maya standing alone in front of the
naked, chained man.

Ammar looks at her imploringly and she struggles to meet his
eyes.

                AMMAR
Your friend is an animal. Please,
help me. Please.

A long beat.

                MAYA
You can help yourself by being
truthful.

The door handle turns. It occurs to Maya that perhaps Daniel
was testing her resilience, too, as Daniel re-enters with a
DOG COLLAR in his hand.

                DANIEL
This is a dog collar.

Daniel unhooks Ammar, snaps the collar and leash around his
neck, as Ammar cries out against the humiliation.

Maya flinches. Daniel is relentless:

                DANIEL (CONT'D)
You determine how I treat you.

Now Daniel drags Ammar on all fours, pulling him by the leash.

                DANIEL (CONT'D)
I'm going to walk you.

Maya watches in horror as Daniel walks Ammar to a far corner
of the room, then leans down to address his victim:

                DANIEL (CONT'D)
What the fuck do you think is going
on, Ammar? Wahleed has already told
me that you know.

At last, Daniel reaches an area of the room where there is a
large wooden box resting on a platform.

                DANIEL (CONT'D)
This box sucks. I'm going to put
you in it.

Ammar tries to speak but can't get a word out.

                DANIEL (CONT'D)
When is the attack?

                AMMAR
        (very softly)
Sunday.

                DANIEL
Sunday? Sunday where? This Sunday
or next Sunday?

Ammar mumbles, almost inaudibly.

                  AMMAR
Monday.

                  DANIEL
Is it Sunday or Monday?

Ammar doesn't answer. The masked men approach.

              DANIEL (CONT'D)
Which day is it? Partial information
is treated as a lie.

                  AMMAR
Saturday.

Beat. The masked men open the box.

              AMMAR (CONT'D)
Sunday!

The guards grab Ammar and carry him to his wooden tomb. He
shouts with his last reserve of energy:

              AMMAR (CONT'D)
Monday!

                  DANIEL
Ammar, which day?

                  AMMAR
        (mumbling)
Monday, Tuesday,

Beat.

              AMMAR (CONT'D)
Thursday.

Beat.

              AMMAR (CONT'D)
Friday.

Daniel slams the box shut. Once again, he's learned nothing.

                        CUT TO:

EXT. KHOBAR TOWERS - SAUDI ARABIA - DAY

ECU: a magazine CLICKS into the receiver of a black assault
rifle.

The weapon, carried by a BEARDED ARAB MAN dressed in street
clothes, rises to shoulder height.

INT. KHOBAR TOWERS - DAY

- The man enters the hallway of the KHOBAR RESIDENTIAL TOWERS

- And immediately opens fire on TWO WESTERN MEN he happens to find inside, killing them both.

TITLE OVER: MAY 29, 2004

- The CRACK of the shots sends the rest of the residents into a panicky, screaming dash for cover

- As he strides quickly down the hall, he finds three other RESIDENTS scrambling for safety, and shoots and kills them all.

                                                    CUT TO:

INT. AMERICAN EMBASSY CIA SECTION - CONFERENCE ROOM

CU TV: news footage of the massacre.

Daniel, Jessica, and Maya look on in defeat. The "Saudi" attack they tried to prevent by pressuring Ammar has occurred.

                         JESSICA
                    (to Daniel)
               Don't worry about the Saudis, they'll
               take care of business.

                         DANIEL
               Yeah, now.

                         JESSICA
               You warned them - they didn't take
               you seriously - this is what happens.
               It's not on you.

                         DANIEL
               Who said that? Zied? Fuck him.
               This is on me. Ammar is on me!!
               And it's on her!!
                    (pointing to Maya)
               We can't let this be a win-win for
               AQ.

                         JESSICA
               No, no, no. You had - what - days -
               brief custody - and an unresponsive
               ally. The way you do this is you
               look ahead. London. Heathrow. Mass
               casualties. That plan is still
               active.

                         MAYA
               Ammar doesn't have a clue about what
               happened.

                         JESSICA
               He knows.

                         MAYA
               How?

                    JESSICA
          You have to be really careful with
          people in KSM's circle - they're
          devious.

                    MAYA
          He's not going to talk about attacks
          on the homeland. He's going to
          withhold operational details on the
          KSM network and probably on bin Laden.
               (flipping her argument)
          But he's been in complete isolation,
          he doesn't know we failed. We can
          tell him anything.

                    DANIEL
          Bluff him?

                    MAYA
          He hasn't slept, Dan. He's clueless.

                                        CUT TO:

EXT. BLACK SITE - AFTERNOON

                    DANIEL (PRE-LAP)
          You don't remember, do you? You -
          me: same same. Bad memory.

While GUARDS move in the deep b.g., Daniel and Maya are seated
at a picnic table with an appetizing spread of Arabic food.

                    DANIEL (PRE-LAP) (CONT'D)
          Short term memory loss is a side
          effect of sleep deprivation. It
          should come back to you.

The Guards bring a prisoner to the table and remove his hood:
Ammar. He stares weakly at the table.

                    AMMAR
               (carefully)
          I don't know. How can I remember?

                    MAYA
          After we kept you awake for 96 hours,
          you gave us names of some of your
          brothers and saved the lives of a
          lot of innocent people.

                    DANIEL
          Which is the smart thing to do, you're
          starting to think for yourself.

Ammar is lost. But the food is tempting.

                    DANIEL (CONT'D)
          Eat up! You earned it.

Ammar eats.

                    DANIEL (CONT'D)
          So you flew via Amman to Kabul to
          hang out with your uncle? Mukhtar.

                    AMMAR
          How did you know that?

                    DANIEL
          I told you man, I know you. Alright,
          you got me - flight manifests. It
          must've been pretty fucked up for
          you guys after 9/11. What did you
          do after the invasion and before you
          went back to Pesh?

                    AMMAR
          After 9/11 I had to choose: fight,
          to protect our turf - or run.

                    DANIEL
               (sympathetic)
          You chose to fight.

Ammar looks Daniel right in the eyes.

                    AMMAR
          I wanted to kill Americans. We tried
          to get into Tora Bora but the bombing
          was too high. We couldn't cross.

                    MAYA
          Sorry, who is the "we" in that
          sentence?

                    AMMAR
          Me and some guys who were hanging
          around at that time.

                    DANIEL
               (casually)
          I can eat with some other dude and
          hook you back up to the ceiling?

                    AMMAR
          Hamza Rabia, Khabab al-Masri, and
          Abu Ahmed.

Maya makes notes on her pad.

                    MAYA
          Who's Abu Ahmed? I've heard of the
          other guys.

                    AMMAR
          He was a computer guy with us at the
          time.
                         (MORE)

                    AMMAR (CONT'D)
          After Tora Bora, I went back to Pesh -
          as you know - and he went North, I
          think, to Kunar.

                    MAYA
          What's his family name?

                    AMMAR
          Abu Ahmed al-Kuwaiti.

                    MAYA
          Abu Ahmed means "father of Ahmed",
          it's a kunya. Ammar, I know the
          difference between a war name and an
          Arabic name.

                    DANIEL
          She got you there, dude.

                    AMMAR
          I swear to you both: I don't know
          his family name. I would have never
          asked him something like that. It's
          not how my uncle worked. My uncle
          told me he worked for bin Laden. I
          did see him, once, about a year ago,
          in Karachi. He read us all a letter
          from the Sheikh.

                    MAYA
          A letter?

                    DANIEL
          What did it say?

Daniel offers Ammar a smoke.

                    DANIEL (CONT'D)
          Cigarette?

Ammar accepts. Daniel's lights it.

                    AMMAR
          It said "Continue the jihad. The
          work will go on for a hundred years."

                                        CUT TO:

INT. AMERICAN EMBASSY - RESEARCH ROOM

We fade into a dimly lit research room, where Maya is alone
watching interrogation video recordings on an array of
monitors. Some of the videos are rough; but most simply
depict two people talking. The video she's watching now shows
a hooded prisoner sitting in a filthy room, the walls smeared
with red stains.

CU SCREEN:

                    SOLDIER INTERROGATOR
          You and I are gonna talk about some
          of the guys in the training camps,
          yeah?

The prisoner sits in a chair. He's hooded, but relaxed.

                    PRISONER
          Ok.

                    SOLDIER INTERROGATOR
          Some of these brothers have done
          some bad things, and what I want to
          do is I want to separate them from
          the people like you.

                    PRISONER
          Definitely, yeah.

                    SOLDIER INTERROGATOR
          There was a guy called Abu Ahmed
          from Kuwait.

                    PRISONER
          Yes, I remember him. A nice guy.

                    SOLDIER INTERROGATOR
          How close was he? What was his
          relationship to the leadership?

                    PRISONER
          I don't know.

                    SOLDIER INTERROGATOR
          Did he eat with you guys - did he
          eat with the good guys - or did he
          eat with the leadership?

                    PRISONER
          I don't know, sir. I have no idea
          about things like that.

                    SOLDIER INTERROGATOR
          Yes you do, you don't need an idea
          about things-

Maya hits *pause* and we see that her desk is filled with open
windows of interrogations: she is analyzing ten videos
simultaneously, comparing them to each other.

INT. RESEARCH ROOM - MOMENTS LATER

She plays another video showing a Turkish prison.

                    TURKISH INTERROGATOR
          When you met with Khalid Sheikh
          Mohammed, was this one of the
          facilitators?

The Interrogator flashes a picture. The prisoner moans.

                    TURKISH INTERROGATOR (CONT'D)
          Is this Abu Ahmed?

                    PRISONER
          Yes.

                                                  CUT TO

INT. RESEARCH ROOM - LATER

She *fast forwards* a video - shot in a Polish facility. The
prisoner appears to be cold.

                    INTERROGATOR
          KSM, your boss.

                    PRISONER
          Mukhtar?

                    INTERROGATOR
          Mukhtar,'potato', you say 'potahto'.
          I say 'fucking KSM', but yeah,
          'Mukhtar.' After Mukhtar was
          captured, what did Abu Ahmed do?

                    PRISONER
          Abu Ahmed, I believe he went to work
          for The Sheikh.

INT. RESEARCH ROOM - LATER

Maya is still in the research room. She's been going at
this for hours and looks fatigued.

CU SCREEN: a different INTERROGATOR from the previous video;
PRISONER is an older man chained to a desk. The exchange is
in Arabic with an English subtitle on the screen:

                    PRISONER
          In Karachi, in 2003 or 2004.

                    INTERROGATOR
          He was carrying a letter from bin
          Laden?

                                                  CUT TO:

INT. RESEARCH ROOM - LATER

Still going, looking exhausted now, Maya manipulates the
controls of yet another video clip with a different
INTERROGATOR and PRISONER. We're now in a Moroccan facility.
The interrogator shows him a photograph of a bearded man.
Henceforth, <u>The Photograph</u>.

                    INTERROGATOR
          Is that him?

                        PRISONER
                 (nods)
            Abu Ahmed.

The interrogator holds The Photograph right in front of the
prisoner's face, allowing us to see it as well.

                        INTERROGATOR
            Say again?

                        PRISONER
            Abu Ahmed. Abu Ahmed. Abu Ahmed.

Freeze frame.

                                              CUT TO:

INT. RESEARCH ROOM - LATER

A Yemeni prison - the dialogue is a mix of French and English:

                        INTERROGATOR
            Abu Ahmed - is he the courier for
            bin Laden?

                        PRISONER
            Who knows who works directly for bin
            Laden? Let's say he's part of the
            mix.

                        INTERROGATOR
            Were there other people who carried
            messages from bin Laden?

                        PRISONER
            Sure.

                        INTERROGATOR
            How many other people?

                        PRISONER
                 (thinking)
            Four or five.

                        INTERROGATOR
            Let's talk about them--

The image freezes.

Maya stares at the screen.

INT. AMERICAN EMBASSY - KITCHEN

Maya is in the kitchen grabbing something to eat.

Jessica, the only other person working this late, walks in,
pours herself some coffee.

                          JESSICA
              How's the needle in the haystack?

                          MAYA
              Fine.

                          JESSICA
              Facilitators come and go, but one
              thing you can count on in life is
              that everyone wants money.

The rivalry is in full bloom. Sometimes it's friendly.
Sometimes it's not so friendly.

                          MAYA
                   (smiling)
              You're assuming that Al Qaeda members
              are motivated by financial rewards.
              They're radicals.

                          JESSICA
                   (bigger smile)
              Correct. You're assuming that greed
              won't override ideology in some of
              the weaker members.

                          MAYA
              Money for walk-ins worked great in
              the cold war, I'll give you that.

                          JESSICA
              Thank you.

                          MAYA
              Just not sure those tactics are
              applicable to the Middle East.

                                             CUT TO:

INT. MAYA'S APARTMENT

Maya hastily throws her clothes and a wig into a suitcase -
the world's fastest packing job -

                                             CUT TO:

EXT. WARSAW SHIPYARD - POLAND - DAY

SUPERIMPOSE: CIA BLACK SITE - WARSAW, POLAND

A sprawling shipyard in an industrial area.

A large MILITARY FRIGATE sits in the harbor. A dark haired
WOMAN and a MAN board the ship.

                                             CUT TO:

INT. FRIGATE - BLACK SITE - POLAND - DAY

At first we don't recognize the woman with heavy makeup
walking down the narrow corridor, and then we realize it's
Maya in disguise.

She enters a vast cavernous hold accompanied by a middle
aged Afghan man, thick shouldered with years of hard
experience in his kind, somewhat sad eyes.

This fatherly man is HAKIM, a former political prisoner in
Afghanistan and one of the CIA's most important assets.

In the galley, a PRISONER is chained to a table. Hakim slides
him The Photograph. The prisoner speaks in Arabic.

                    HAKIM
               (translating)
          He says he looks like Abu Ahmed.

                    MAYA
          Who did he work for?

Hakim translates. Then the prisoner speaks.

                    HAKIM
               (translating)
          It was mostly with Abu Faraj - they
          were always together.

                    MAYA
          What did he do for Faraj?

                    HAKIM
               (translating)
          He carried messages from Faraj to
          bin Laden and from bin Laden back to
          Faraj.

Maya leans into Hakim -

                    MAYA
          We need to ask him something to see
          if he's telling the truth. We don't
          know if he really knew Faraj.

Hakim speaks to the prisoner.

                    HAKIM
          He just told me the names of all of
          Faraj's children. I think he's
          telling the truth.

                                             CUT TO:

INT. AMERICAN EMBASSY - CIA SECTION

Maya is pitching Bradley in his office. Bradley sits with
his feet up on his desk, holding The Photograph.

Daniel is slouched on the couch in back.

Jessica is perched on the arm of the couch, bare legs crossed.
Bradley notices.

Maya stands.

>   MAYA
>   Twenty detainees recognize that photo
>   of Abu Ahmed. They say he's part of
>   the inner circle of guys who were
>   hanging out in Afghanistan pre-9/11.
>   (beat)
>   A lot of them say that after 9/11,
>   he went to work for KSM.
>   (beat)
>   When KSM got captured, he went to
>   work for Abu Faraj, primarily as a
>   courier from Faraj to bin Laden.

>   BRADLEY
>   Well, that's good. You still-

>   MAYA
>   Yeah, we don't know if Abu is on the
>   outside of the network - part of a
>   series of cutouts and dead drops -
>   or if he has a direct connection to
>   bin Laden. Does bin Laden invite
>   him into the living room and hand
>   him a letter directly? Or is Abu
>   just the last guy in a long line of
>   couriers, so that's why everybody
>   knows him?

>   BRADLEY
>   That's not all you don't know. You
>   don't have his true name, and you
>   don't have a clue of where he is.

>   MAYA
>   We know that he's important. The
>   fact that everybody's heard of Abu
>   Ahmed but nobody will tell me where
>   he is suggests that.

>   BRADLEY
>   Maybe. Detainees could withhold his
>   location for any number of reasons.
>   Perhaps they don't know; perhaps
>   this Abu is just a cover story and
>   he's really a fucking unicorn. The
>   withholding doesn't reveal what you
>   want it to - does it?

>   MAYA
>   No.

                    BRADLEY
     And if you did find him, you don't
     know that he'd be with bin Laden.

                    DANIEL
     We don't know what we don't know.

                    BRADLEY
          (to Daniel)
     What the fuck is that supposed to
     mean?

                    DANIEL
     It's a tautology.

                    BRADLEY
          (back to Maya)
     Listen, not one single detainee has
     said that he's located with the big
     guy, just that he delivers messages.
     Am I wrong?

                    MAYA
     No.

                    BRADLEY
     No. It's still good work. Let me
     know when you've got some actionable
     intelligence, preferably something
     that leads to a strike.

                                             CUT TO:

EXT. TAVISTOCK SQUARE - LONDON - EARLY MORNING

The city is in full swing on this bright mid-summer morning.

CARS and BUSES roll through the crowded streets.

INT./EXT. DOUBLE DECKER BUS

TITLE OVER: LONDON - JULY 7, 2005

Passengers inside the bus read newspapers, listen to music...
another ordinary day.

Then, the bus explodes!

                                             CUT TO:

CU: TV SCREEN

File footage of the aftermath:

                    REPORTER (O.S.)
     This is what remains of the #10 bus,
     which was traveling through Tavistock
     Square...

INT. AMERICAN EMBASSY CIA SECTION - STATION CHIEF'S OFFICE - NIGHT

Joseph Bradley sits at his desk. The weight of the world on his shoulders.

On the television in the background, the news report continues, showing disaster footage of PEOPLE bloodied, screaming.

                                                    CUT TO:

EXT. BLACK SITE - AFGHANISTAN

The war on terror is growing and spreading, like an octopus, throughout the base. We trace the new tentacles of the CIA facility - more hangars, vehicles, PEOPLE moving to and fro.

                    REPORTER   (O.S.)
               All around, groups of Londoners are
               standing on corners asking themselves
               what has happened here, and who could
               possibly have done this?

We find Daniel trying to catch a moment of solitude...eating an ice cream cone and standing in front of a makeshift cage filled with wild MONKEYS.

The monkeys are watching Daniel intently, their hands gripping the wire cage. Daniel playfully feeds them some of his ice cream.

A CIA GUARD approaches Daniel

                    CIA GUARD
                 (re: the monkeys)
               You Agency guys are twisted. The
               detainee is ready.

Daniel nods, weary. Then a monkey reaches through the bars and steals the remainder of Daniel's ice cream cone.

He looks at the monkey and laughs.

                                                    CUT TO:

EXT. ISLAMABAD TRAFFIC - YEARS LATER

Rain pelts the brown city, turning the gutter water black.

                    MAYA (PRE-LAP)
               I want you to understand that I know
               you. I have been following you and
               studying you for a long time. I
               chased you in Lahore.

We find Maya entering the gates of a Pakistani prison. The weather makes the place seem especially bleak.

SUPERIMPOSE: MILITARY DETENTION CENTER - ISLAMABAD, PAKISTAN

INT. PAKISTANI DETENTION AREA - CONTINUOUS

HASSAN GHUL, Al Qaeda financier, sits manacled to a desk.

> MAYA
> I had you picked up instead of killing
> you because you're not a violent man
> and you don't deserve to die.

> GHUL
> Thank you.

> MAYA
> But you do have deep ties to Al Qaeda
> that I want to ask you about before
> you get sent to your next location,
> which might be Israel.

Ghul looks ashen.

> MAYA (CONT'D)
> However, depending on how candid you
> are today, I may be able to keep you
> in Pakistan.

> GHUL
> What do you want to know?

> MAYA
> I'm going to ask you a series of
> questions based on your knowledge of
> Al Qaeda and your position as key
> financier for the organization.

> GHUL
> I have dealt with the mukhabarat, I
> have no wish to be tortured again.
> Ask me a question, I can answer it.

> MAYA
> What can you tell me about Atiyah
> Abd al-Rahman.

> GHUL
> He works for Zawahiri. He's in charge
> of military tactics.

> MAYA
> In what context have you ever heard
> the name Abu Ahmed?

> GHUL
> He works for Faraj and bin Laden.
> He is his most trusted courier.

Maya works hard to hide how pleased she is to have this
confirmation. She's not entirely successful.

                              MAYA
             What makes you say that?

                              GHUL
             He brought me many messages from the
             Sheikh.

                              MAYA
             Where did you last see him, and where
             is he now?

                              GHUL
             You will never find him.

                              MAYA
             Why is that?

                              GHUL
             Even I couldn't find him. He always
             contacted me out of the blue. He is
             one of the disappeared ones.

                                                  CUT TO:

EXT. GARDEN COMPLEX - PAKISTAN - DAY

Pakistani families enjoy a fine summer day.

INT. GARDEN VILLA

A BOMB is being strapped to a MAN'S leg by a PAKISTANI
POLICEMAN.

                         PAKISTANI POLICEMAN
                    (in Urdu)
             You know how this works?

The man is terrified.

                         PAKISTANI POLICEMAN (CONT'D)
             Just act naturally.

The Policeman finishes securing the bomb, and sends the man
out the door (who we will later deduce is Abu Faraj's
courier).

                                                  CUT TO:

EXT. GARDEN COMPLEX - DAY

Faraj's Courier walks past playing children... while from a
nearby tower, Daniel observes.

After a moment, ABU FARAJ, who we recognize from his
photograph, appears at the south end of the park. Faraj
walks in the direction of his courier, noting his
surroundings:

CHILDREN playing.

Several people in BLACK BURKHAS.

BRIGHT SUN.

At last Faraj reaches an open area where he can see his courier face to face.

They exchange a nervous glance that conveys the danger: It's a trap. Faraj spins to flee, but it's too late.

The black BURKHAS descend on him. It turns out they are heavily armed Pakistani agents. From on high, Daniel watches his captured prey.

CUT TO:

EXT. BLACK SITE - AFGHANISTAN - DAY

Daniel and an armed guard escort a hooded and handcuffed Faraj to his cell.

> DANIEL
> What do you like? Bob Marley?
> Reggae? Egyptian music? Just let me
> know, if there's music you like, I
> can make a call.

INT. INTERROGATION AREA - CONTINUOUS

Daniel and the guards take Faraj to a cell laced with barbed wire and lock him inside.

> DANIEL
> Can I be honest with you? I'm bad
> news. I'm not your friend. I'm not
> gonna help you. I'm gonna break
> you.

Beat.

> DANIEL (CONT'D)
> I've done it before.
>   (Faraj dozes, weak)
> Hey, wake up. You haven't eaten in
> 18 hours, we've got to keep your
> energy up. You hungry?

CUT TO:

INT. CELL

Guards force feed Faraj through a feeding tube.

CUT TO:

INT. AMERICAN EMBASSY CIA SECTION - MAYA'S CUBICLE - DAY

Bradley approaches Maya at her cubicle.

                    BRADLEY
          You're in luck, I got you a one-on-
          one with Faraj.

                    MAYA
          Seriously? Thank you.

                    BRADLEY
          Don't thank me until you hear what I
          want for it.

He drops a folder on her desk.

                    BRADLEY (CONT'D)
          I want you to take care of all of
          this before your favorite subject.

                    MAYA
          Deal.

                    BRADLEY
          Don't you want to see what's in the
          folder?

                    MAYA
          You want family ties, financial
          networks, media sources, disgruntled
          employees, imminent threats, homeland
          plots,

                    BRADLEY
               (walking away)
          Thank you.

                    MAYA
          Foreign cells, health status, trade
          craft, recruiting tactics -- anything
          else?

                                        CUT TO:

INT. INTERROGATION ROOM - MORNING

Both Maya and Faraj look tired. This has been going on for
hours.

                    MAYA
          A lot of brothers told us Abu Ahmed
          was bin Laden's courier and that he
          worked very closely with you.

                    FARAJ
          You're thinking of Abu Khalid.

                    MAYA
          Who?

                    FARAJ
          Al Buluchi. My courier for the
          Sheikh.

                    MAYA
          Okay, so you're telling me that all
          the other brothers are wrong, and
          there's some famous Buluchi guy that
          is working for you and bin Laden
          that I've never even heard of?

                    FARAJ
          Why should you have heard of him?

                    MAYA
          What does this Buluchi guy look like?

                    FARAJ
          Tall, long white beard, thin. He
          uses a cane.

                    MAYA
          Kind of like Gandolf?

                    FARAJ
          Who?

                    MAYA
          When was the last time you saw him?

                    FARAJ
          A month ago, in Karachi, but I don't
          know where he is now. Sometimes I
          wouldn't even see him, he would just
          tell me where to leave the messages.

                    MAYA
          I don't believe you.

The GUARD in the room with them leans forward and SLAPS Faraj
across the face.

Faraj's expression doesn't change and Maya herself remains
flat and steady, unmoved by the violence.

She's not quite the same young lady she was a few years ago.

                    MAYA (CONT'D)
          You're not being fulsome in your
          replies.

                    FARAJ
          You can't force me to tell you
          something I don't know.

                    MAYA
          You do realize this is not a normal
          prison.
                              (MORE)

                         MAYA (CONT'D)
              You determine how you are treated,
              and your life will be very
              uncomfortable until you give me
              information I need.

The guard slaps Faraj again. Faraj is impassive.

                                                  CUT TO:

INT.   INTERROGATION ROOM - LATER

Maya looks on impassively as Faraj is subjected to harsh
treatment.

                                                  CUT TO:

INT. BLACK SITE - BATHROOM

Maya is retching in the stall.

                                                  CUT TO:

EXT. BLACK SITE - PRE-DAWN

Maya walks around the facility, quiet at this hour, and finds
another insomniac, Daniel, by the monkey cage. The cage is
empty.

                         MAYA
              Faraj is completely denying knowing
              Abu Ahmed, and that's using every
              measure we have.

                         DANIEL
              He's either going to withhold or die
              from the pressure you're putting on
              him.

                         MAYA
              Do you want to take a run at him?

                         DANIEL
              No.

                         MAYA
              No? Since when?

                         DANIEL
              You know, I've been meaning to tell
              you: I'm getting outta here.

                         MAYA
              What? You okay?

                         DANIEL
              I'm fine. I've just seen too many
              guys naked.
                              (MORE)

                    DANIEL (CONT'D)
          It's gotta be over a hundred at this
          point. I need to go do something
          normal for awhile.

                    MAYA
          Like what?

                    DANIEL
          Go to Washington, do the dance, see
          how that environment works.
                    (beat)
          You should come with me. Be my number
          two. You're looking a little strung
          out yourself.

Maya looks at Dan. No longer the man he once was. She
doesn't hide her disappointment.

                    MAYA
          I'm not going to find Abu Ahmed from
          D.C.

They both look at the empty cage, clocking the irony.

                    DANIEL
          They killed my monkeys.
          Something about an escape. Can you
          fucking believe that?

                    MAYA
          Sorry, Dan.

                    DANIEL
          Look, Maya, you gotta be really
          careful with detainees now. The
          politics are changing and you don't
          want to be the last one holding a
          dog collar when the oversight
          committee comes.

                    MAYA
          I know.

                    DANIEL
          And watch your back when you get
          back to Pakistan. Everyone knows
          you there now.

                                             CUT TO:

EXT. ISLAMABAD - NIGHT

Back in Pakistan, the country has indeed changed to a more
militarized police state, and as we establish the new
environment, we find Maya's grey sedan...

EXT. ISLAMABAD - NEAR THE MARRIOTT HOTEL - NIGHT

The car pulls up to a checkpoint manned by PAKISTANI POLICE.
The Policeman look at the car - look at the plate - the plate
is diplomatic - they walk around the car and stop at the
window - shine their bright light right into Maya's eyes.

A POLICEMAN motions for her to roll down her window.

                    POLICEMAN
          Where are you going?

                    MAYA
          To the Marriott. I assume you noticed
          the dip plates.

                    POLICEMAN
          But you have a bag -

The policeman motions to a DUFFEL BAG resting on the rear
seat.

                    MAYA
          It's a gym bag.

Maya does not get out of the car. She stares at him
defiantly. He advances forward a bit. She rolls up her
window, flicks the door lock, and starts dialing her cell
phone.

The policeman walks away to rejoin his group. The police
confer. The original policeman returns, this time with
several other cops. They knock on the glass. Hard.

Maya stares straight ahead.

                                        CUT TO:

INT. MARRIOTT HOTEL RESTAURANT - NIGHT

Jessica is waiting at the table in a beautifully appointed
room.

SUPERIMPOSE: MARRIOTT HOTEL - ISLAMABAD, PAKISTAN - SEPTEMBER
20, 2008

Maya walks in, flustered.

                    MAYA
          Fucking checkpoints.

Maya sits down, absorbed in her Blackberry.

                    JESSICA
          Maya?

                    MAYA
          Yeah.

                    JESSICA
          We're socializing. Be social.

Maya puts away her blackberry.

                    MAYA
               (halfheartedly)
          Okay.

                    JESSICA
          Look, I know Abu Ahmed is your baby,
          but it's time to cut the umbilical
          cord.

                    MAYA
          No, it's not.

                    JESSICA
          So Faraj went south on you - it
          happens. There are still cells in
          London and Spain planning the next
          round of attacks.

                    MAYA
          I can work on it at the same time -
          plus I think it's a good thing that
          he lied.

                    JESSICA
          No, not at the expense of protecting
          the homeland, you can't. Wait a
          minute, why is it a good thing?

                    MAYA
          You sound just like Bradley. He
          doesn't believe in my lead either.
               (beat)
          It's a good thing because the fact
          that Faraj withheld on Abu Ahmed is
          revealing. The only other thing he
          lied about was the location of bin
          Laden himself. That means Faraj
          thinks Abu Ahmed in as important to
          protect as bin Laden. That confirms
          my lead.

                    JESSICA
          Or it's confirmation bias.
               (beat)
          We're all just worried about you,
          okay? Is that okay to say?

Maya rubs her eyes, not liking where the conversation is
going. She forces a smile.

                    JESSICA (CONT'D)
          Where's Jack?

                    MAYA
          He's probably stuck in some check-
          point somewhere.

                    JESSICA
          You two hooked up yet?

                    MAYA
          Hello, I work with him. I'm not
          that girl, that fucks. It's
          unbecoming.

                    JESSICA
          So? A little foolin' around wouldn't
          hurt you.
                    (beat)
          So no boyfriend. Do you have any
          friends at all?

She doesn't. Jessica's phone rings -

                    JESSICA (CONT'D)
          It's Jack.
                    (into phone)
          Hey - that's okay -

SUDDENLY, AN EXPLOSION RIPS THROUGH THE RESTAURANT.

-- SHATTERS THE WINDOWS

-- DESTROYS TABLES AND LIGHTS

-- MAYA, JESSICA, AND OTHERS TOSSED TO THE GROUND, SOME
FATALLY.

--SMOKE FILLS THE ROOM

As alarms wail, Maya struggles to her feet, grabs Jessica by
the arm, and they stumble to safety.

INT. MARRIOTT - DINING ROOM

Toward the destroyed kitchen, helping each other over
obstacles, twisted metal, gaps in the concrete, etc, past
injured workers and burning flames.

INT. MARRIOTT HOTEL - KITCHEN - LATER

They continue moving through the debris as the smoke
intensifies.

They find each other's hands and grab tightly.

                                             CUT TO:

C.U.: TV SCREEN

The destroyed Marriott.

                    REPORTER (O.S.)
          The blast left a crater 10 meters
          wide in front of the hotel. The
          Marriott, one of the most popular
          destinations for locals and
          Westerners...

FADE TO BLACK

EXT. MOUNTAINOUS TRIBAL AREA - PAKISTAN - DAY

We're high above the wild hinterlands of the Hindu Kush,
gliding over the rocky slopes and the pine forests.

SUPERIMPOSE: TRIBAL TERRITORIES, NORTHERN PAKISTAN

We move from peak to peak until we find a remote valley, and
we zoom down... and nestled in the valley we can just make
out the barest outlines of a tiny village of mud huts.

INT. TRIBAL VILLAGE HUT

Now we are inside a hut and we've shifted to the perspective
of a hand held camera, as if someone inside this stone age
interior is filming on our behalf, and we see a hard floor,
thin gaps in the walls, and FIVE TRIBAL ELDERS talking
casually, eating and drinking tea.

We pan across the weathered faces, long beards, and see a
video recorder resting on a ledge.

                                            CUT TO:

INT. AMERICAN EMBASSY CIA SECTION - ISLAMABAD - DAY

Jessica strides excitedly, almost breaking into a run, through
the warren of cubicles that lead to Maya's desk.

INT. AMERICAN EMBASSY CIA SECTION - MAYA'S CUBICLE - DAY

Jessica beaming as she approaches Maya.

                    JESSICA
          The Jords have a mole!

                    MAYA
          What?

Jessica pops a CD into Maya's computer, loads a file that
plays the same video clip we have just seen.

                    JESSICA
          He made this video to prove his bona
          fides.

                    MAYA
          Shut the fuck up!

The camera stops on one man, BALAWI.

                    JESSICA
               (pointing)
          Humam Khalil al-Balawi, he's a
          Jordanian doctor. He's really
          motivated.

Maya practically bolts out of her chair. Together, they
start walking towards Bradley's office -

                    MAYA
          This could be it!

                    JESSICA
          This is it.

INT. AMERICAN EMBASSY CIA SECTION - STATION CHIEF'S OFFICE -
CONTINUOUS

Bradley has just finished watching the video. Maya and
Jessica are in his office waiting for his verdict.

                    JESSICA
          He's right there in the inner circle.

                    BRADLEY
          I don't buy it. Didn't you tell me
          yourself nobody turns on Al Qaeda?

                    JESSICA
          The Jords worked him for a year.
          Dinners, money. They've convinced
          him that it's his patriotic duty to
          turn on Al Qaeda and get rich doing
          it.

                    BRADLEY
          Yeah, so the Jords say.

                    MAYA
               (to Bradley)
          You're right. We can't rely on the
          Jords. We have to evaluate him face
          to face.

                    JESSICA
               (catching on)
          He may not be that smart. He may be
          full of shit - but we have to talk
          to him to find out.

                    MAYA
          The key is to meet him so we can
          figure out for ourselves what he can
          actually do.

                         BRADLEY
            He really asked for a dialysis
            machine? You can fill the damn thing
            with poison.

                                              CUT TO:

INT. AMERICAN EMBASSY ISLAMABAD - BRIEFING ROOM - NIGHT

Maya and a few analysts are watching TV - President-elect
Obama is being interviewed on 60 Minutes when Jessica comes
into the room with disappointing news -

                         JESSICA
            The meeting with Balawi is off. He
            can't come here to Islamabad.

                         MAYA
            Can't or won't?

                         JESSICA
            He's not going to travel - security
            risk -

The TV interview with Obama reaches the subject of enhanced
interrogation, and the women pause to listen to the President-
elect declare, "America does not torture."

Then they continue:

                         JESSICA (CONT'D)
            He wants us to go to him. He'll
            meet in Miram Sha or the tribals.

                         MAYA
            He knows we're white. You'll get
            kidnapped up there.

DAVID, an analyst, adds his two cents to the conversation -

                         DAVID
            We could do it somewhere else -
            Germany, or the UK? He's got a clean
            passport.

                         JESSICA
            He's not going to travel out of Al
            Qaeda territory.

                         DAVID
            And you're not going to him.

                         JESSICA
            I'm not. Believe me.
                 (pause)
            We're stuck.

                         DAVID
          What about Camp Chapman? Afghanistan.
          That could be safe territory.

                                             CUT TO:

EXT. CAMP CHAPMAN CIA COMPOUND - KHOST, AFGHANISTAN - DAY

We survey the sprawling base from above.

SUPERIMPOSE: CAMP CHAPMAN - KHOST, AFGHANISTAN

Helicopters and Humvees traverse the base.

INT. CAMP CHAPMAN - KITCHEN - MORNING

Jessica applies icing to a birthday cake as she cradles a
SATELLITE PHONE.

                         JESSICA
                    (into phone)
          This may be going overboard, but I
          baked him a cake!

                         MAYA O.S.
          Muslim's don't celebrate with cake.

                         JESSICA
          Don't be so literal. Everyone likes
          cake. It's not too late for you to
          come, you know. It will be fun.

                                             CUT TO:

INT. AMERICAN EMBASSY - PREDATOR BAY

Maya sits in front of a series of monitors. She watches a
live Predator feed.

                         MAYA
          I don't want to be a straphangar.
          It's your show. You were the first
          to see the potential in this.

                         JESSICA (O.S.)
          Come on! We've got lots of wine!

The target on Maya's monitor disappears in a puff of smoke.

                         MAYA
          Cool. Bring me back a bottle.

                         JESSICA (O.S.)
          I will.

                                             CUT TO:

INT. DINING AREA

Jessica pours two glasses of wine and raises a toast to her colleague, JOHN.

>   JESSICA
>   Not to get technical, but this guy
>   is actually the first big break we've
>   had since 9/11. To big breaks and
>   the little people that make them
>   happen.

Clink.

>   JESSICA (CONT'D)
>   So far, everything he's said we've
>   cross checked and it's proved legit...
>   and I think the money is persuasive.
>   25 million dollars?! That buys a
>   new life.

>   JOHN
>   Do you think he might be exaggerating
>   his access?

>   JESSICA
>   Possibly. But Al Qaeda needs doctors
>   *and they are short staffed* and that
>   could explain his rise. In six months
>   to a year, if he doesn't fuck up, he
>   could be called in to treat bin Laden.
>   And at that moment, with 25 mil on
>   the table, I think he gives up the
>   Big Man. And if he doesn't, we kill
>   him.

                                                  CUT TO:

EXT. CAMP CHAPMAN CIA COMPOUND - AFTERNOON

The same gathering as the day before, waiting under the merciless sun.

SUPERIMPOSE: DECEMBER 30, 2009

Jessica turns to her crew, which includes LAUREN, a young operative, ZIED, a Jordanian intelligence agent, and the base's CIA SECURITY GUARD, among others. They rehearse the impending meeting.

>   JESSICA
>   So John?
>   (John turns to her)
>   When he arrives, I'll set the tone,
>   and then I'll flip it to you - and
>   you'll talk about asset protection.

>   JOHN
>   Roger that.

                    JESSICA
          Then Lauren, I know you want to get
          some questions in there - but give
          Balawi time after John speaks. We'll
          cover the basics and have his birthday
          cake, then we'll get to the nitty
          gritty.

Jessica turns to Zied.

                    JESSICA (CONT'D)
          Is that order okay, or do you want
          to introduce everyone?

                    ZIED
          I'll introduce you, and you introduce
          your team. He knows this is a high
          level meeting.

                    SECURTY GUARD
          Quick question: all is taking place
          inside our main building?

                    JESSICA
          Right. And Lauren? Washington will
          want real time updates so please
          stay on top of that. Be concise.
          The Director is in the loop. And I
          wouldn't be surprised if he doesn't
          update the President.

                    LAUREN
          Yeah, I'm on it.

They take in the possibilities.

                    JESSICA
          Now, I just need to get Balawi's ass
          down here.

LATER -

Waiting and waiting. No cars approach. The sun beats down.

                                        CUT TO:

EXT. CAMP CHAPMAN - ROAD TO SOUTH GATE

Several hundred yards before the Camp entrance is a beat-up
SEDAN. The car pulls up to the checkpoint but doesn't
proceed.

                    JESSICA
               (to the Security Gyard)
          Why are there gate guards there? We
          talked about this, no one is supposed
          to be there when my source arrives.
          You might have spooked him already!

                         SECURTY GUARD
               Procedures only work if we follow
               them every time.

                         JESSICA
               This time is different - I'm sorry I
               can't explain, but it's for a good
               cause.

                         SECURTY GUARD
               Look, I'm responsible for everyone's
               safety, okay? It's not just about
               you.

                         JESSICA
               I just need them to go away for a
               minute. You can search him as soon
               as he gets here.

The Security Guard pauses, then into his radio:

                         SECURTY GUARD
                    (into radio)
               All stations, go ahead and stand
               down.

                         CHECKPOINT GUARD
                    (over radio)
               Roger.

EXT. CAMP CHAPMAN - GUARD POST

The guards move away from their post. The sedan drives past
the gate into a maze of barriers. We follow the car as it
navigates the maze of HESCO barriers, kicking up a cloud of
dust.

EXT. CAMP CHAPMAN - CIA COMPOUND

Jessica runs back to her team and flashes a thumbs up.

She smiles and pulls out her phone, sending a text.

ECU: PHONE TEXT:

He's here. Brb

Maya:

Cool!

The car navigates the second set of barriers.

INT. AMERICAN EMBASSY - MAYA'S CUBICLE - SECONDS LATER

Maya types on her computer:

Wassup you talking yet

?

EXT. CAMP CHAPMAN - CIA COMPOUND

Jessica looks up to see the car approaching and puts the
phone back in her pocket. The sedan is now 50 yards away.

> SECURTY GUARD
> Okay, he's coming. We're gonna search
> him when he gets here.

Everyone prepares. The car gets closer and closer, a driver
in front and a passenger in back.

INT. AMERICAN EMBASSY - MAYA'S CUBICLE

Maya texts again:

?

Answer when you can.

EXT. CAMP CHAPMAN - CIA COMPOUND

The sedan pulls to a stop. A BLACKWATER GUARD taps on the
backseat window. Balawi exits on the passenger side. His
free hand is in his pocket.

> BLACKWATER GUARD
> (to the other guard)
> Is he supposed to limp like that?

> SECURTY GUARD
> Take your hand out of your pocket!
> Hey!

> BALAWI
> Allahu Akbar, Allahu Akbar

> BLACKWATER GUARD
> (raising his M4)
> Get you hand out of your pocket!

> BALAWI
> Allahu Akbar.

Jessica's smile fades

And Balawi detonates a suicide vest hidden under this jacket
and the resulting shrapnel storm pulps the crowd, massacring
them all -

                                            CUT TO:

INT. AMERICAN EMBASSY ISLAMABAD, CIA SECTION - CONTINUOUS

Maya looks at her computer screen. She sees her last instant
message..And waits for a response.

Beat.

Maya looks up, concern on her face.

CUT TO:

EXT. CAMP CHAPMAN - DAY

The explosion smoke still hovers over Camp Chapman. News
reporting of the attack plays over the horrific image.

INT. AMERICAN EMBASSY CIA SECTION - MAYA'S CUBICLE - LATER

Maya huddles on the floor under the corner of her desk.

INT. MAYA'S CUBICLE - LATER

The office has thinned out, and most people have gone home
for the day. Maya is crouched in the corner. A wounded
animal. Jeremy, the case officer from the conference room,
approaches and gives Maya a computer disc.

                    JEREMY
          You okay?

No response.

                    JEREMY (CONT'D)
          I didn't think this day could get
          any worse, but bad news from Saudi
          intelligence. The courier guy, Abu
          Ahmed, is dead. It's a detainee
          video.

Maya still fighting to contain her grief, takes the file as
an almost welcome distraction. She puts the disc into her
computer and hits play.

CU COMPUTER SCREEN: A PRISONER being interviewed by a CIA
CASE OFFICER holds the photo of Abu Ahmed we've seen so many
times.

                    PRISONER
          He's dead, in Afghanistan, 2001. I
          buried him with my own hands.

                    INTERROGATOR
          Where?

                    PRISONER
          Kabul.

Maya stares at the screen.

                    MAYA
          I don't believe this.

                         JEREMY
             Sorry, Maya, I always liked this
             lead.

Jeremy leaves Maya at her computer.

She continues to stare at the screen.

INT. MAYA'S CUBICLE - NIGHT

Maya is still by herself.

Her friend Jack approaches -

                         JACK
                    (consoling)
             Hey. Sorry, I just got here. What
             are you gonna do?

                         MAYA
             I'm going to smoke everybody involved
             in this op, and then I'm going to
             kill bin Laden.

Off the darkness in her eyes we -

FADE TO BLACK

                                             CUT TO:

INT. AMERICAN EMBASSY ISLAMABAD - CIA SECTION - A YEAR LATER

The staff has gathered to hear a word from the boss in a
large conference room; it's packed shoulder to shoulder with
dozens of people, including Maya, Jim, Jack, Hakim, and
Bradley at the front.

GEORGE WRIGHT, Chief of the Afghanistan Pakistan Department,
has just flown in from D.C. A big man, striding quickly into
the room with the street roll of the Bronx projects he grew
up in, George looks ready for a brawl.

                         GEORGE
             I want to make something absolutely
             clear. If you thought there was
             some secret cell somewhere working
             Al Qaeda, I want *you to know that
             you're wrong.* This is it. There's
             no working group coming to the rescue.

He stares at his staff.

                         GEORGE (CONT'D)
             There's nobody else, hidden away on
             some other floor. There is just us.
             And we are failing. We're spending
             billions of dollars. People are
             dying. We're still no closer to
             defeating our enemy.

Pacing now:

> GEORGE (CONT'D)
> They attacked us on land in 98, by
> sea in 2000, and from the air in
> 2001. They murdered three thousand
> of our citizens in cold blood, and
> they've slaughtered our forward
> deployed. And what the fuck have we
> done about it?
> (yelling now)
> What have we done?
> (pause)
> We have twenty leadership names and
> we've only eliminated four of them.

Beat.

> GEORGE (CONT'D)
> I want targets! Do your fucking
> jobs, bring me people to kill!

INT. AMERICAN EMBASSY CIA SECTION - LATER

The office has grown bigger and busier and the cubicle maze
is filled with many new faces of young agents excited to be
in Pakistan.

Sitting alone at her desk we find Maya just as she's finishing
a report. She gets up, crosses the room and goes to the
desk of a young woman who reminds us in her idealistic
enthusiasm of the way Maya was six years ago. This is DEBBIE.

> DEBBIE
> Hi. I painstakingly combed through
> everything in the system and found
> this.

She hands Maya a file.

> DEBBIE (CONT'D)
> It's him. He was one of ten names
> on a watch list sent to us by the
> Moroccans after 9/11: Ibrahim Sayeed.
> They told us to watch out for him,
> apparently they think his whole family
> and extended family is bad and has
> ties to KSM.
> (beat)
> He was picked up for fake papers and
> a doctored exit visa leaving
> Afghanistan, traveling through Morocco
> en route to Kuwait. Abu Ahmed al-
> Kuwaiti. This must be Abu Ahmed.

                    MAYA
          Doesn't matter, but I wish I had
          that five years ago. How come I
          never saw it before?

                    DEBBIE
          Nobody saw it, most likely. There
          was a lot of white noise after 9/11,
          countries wanting to help out, we
          got millions of tips and...
               (shrugs)
          Things got lost in the shuffle.
          Human error.

Maya turns her attention back to the WHITE BOARD and as Debbie
keeps talking we follow Maya's gaze across the row of MUG
SHOTS of Al Qaeda personnel. While a few of the men are
African or are distinctive looking for other reasons, most
of them look fairly similar in that they're all wearing the
same type of clothes and have the same trademark long gnarly
beards.

                    DEBBIE (CONT'D)
               (pressing on)
          Anyway I thought you should know
          about it.
               (plus)
          I just want to say I've heard a lot
          about you. You inspired me to come
          to Pakistan.

Maya's eyes narrow. She keeps looking at the WHITE BOARD

                    DEBBIE (CONT'D)
          Maybe you'll let me buy you a kabob
          sometime?

                    MAYA
               (distractedly)
          Don't eat out. It's too dangerous.

Maya stares at the Al Quaeda mugshots - a thought crosses
her mind.

                                             CUT TO:

INT. AMERICAN EMBASSY CIA SECTION - BRIEFING ROOM - NIGHT

Maya on the speaker phone to Daniel. We intercut. Daniel
is now a suit in Langley.

                    MAYA
               (over speaker)
          Dan, Debbie found Abu Ahmed!

                    DANIEL
          Fuck. Really?

                    MAYA
              (over speaker)
          He was in the files this whole time.
          The family name is Sayeed.

                    DANIEL
          Ok, but he's dead. So doesn't that
          make him a little less interesting
          to you?

                    MAYA O.S.
          He may not be. We now know that Abu
          Ahmed is one of eight brothers. All
          the brothers in the family look alike.
          Three of them went to Afghanistan.
          Isn't it possible that when the three
          eldest brothers grew beards in
          Afghanistan, they started to look
          alike? I think the one calling
          himself Abu Ahmed is still alive.
          The picture we've been using is wrong.
          It's of his older brother, Habeeb.
          He's the one that's is dead.

                    DANIEL
          Okay, what are you basing this on?

INT. BRIEFING ROOM - CONTINUOUS

                    MAYA
          We have no intercepts about Abu Ahmed
          dying. We just have a detainee who
          buried somebody who looked like Abu
          Ahmed. But if somebody as important
          as Abu Ahmed had died, they'd be
          talking about it online in chat rooms
          all over the place. Plus, the
          detainee said that Habeeb died in
          2001. We know that Abu Ahmed was
          alive then, trying to get into Tora
          Bora with Ammar. That means it's
          probably one of the other brothers
          that's dead.

                    DANIEL O.S.
          In other words, you want it to be
          true.

                    MAYA
          Yes, I fucking want it to be true.

Maya slams the desk.

                    DANIEL O.S.
          Calm down.

Beat.

                    MAYA
          I am calm.

                    DANIEL O.S.
          State your request.

                    MAYA
          Move heaven and earth and bring me
          this fucking Sayeed family's phone
          number.

                                        CUT TO:

INT. CIA HEADQUARTERS, COUNTER TERRORISM CENTER DIRECTOR -
LANGLEY, VA. - DAY

A dark (window shades down) executive office, where in the
shadows a white American man in a nice suit is kneeling on a
prayer rug and saying the Islamic daily prayers.

Daniel waits as the man recites the prayers and presses his
pale forehead to the carpet. This is WOLF. He is the head
of the agency's COUNTER TERRORISM CENTER (George's boss).

                    DANIEL
          As-Salamu alaykum.

                    WOLF
          Alaykum salam.

                    DANIEL
          I need a couple hundred thousand.
          Four max.

                    WOLF
          Where you gonna get that?

                    DANIEL
          From you.

                    WOLF
          You think so?

                    DANIEL
          This could crack open the facilitator
          Maya's been looking for by giving us
          a phone number.
               (beat)
          She's your killer, Wolf. You put
          her on the field.
               (reciting a phrase
                from the KORAN, in
                Arabic, then loosely
                translating)
          *Allah rewards those who strive and
          fight over those that sit behind a
          desk.*

WOLF nods. If the blatant attempt to play on his Muslim belief bothers him, he doesn't show it at all.

> WOLF
> As you know, Abu Ghraib and Gitmo
> fucked us. The detainee program is
> now fly paper. We got senators
> jumping out of our asses, and the
> Director is very concerned. They
> will not stop until they have a body.

There it is. The quid pro quo. There's a reason he's called The Wolf.

Daniel considers all that he'll go through if he volunteers to be the fall guy for the controversial program.

> DANIEL
> I ran it. I'll defend it.

                                                    CUT TO:

INT. KUWAITI UNDERGROUND HOOKER BAR - NIGHT

SUPERIMPOSE: KUWAIT CITY, KUWAIT

Daniel and a KUWAITI BUSINESS MAN in a suit are drinking and ogling the RUSSIAN GIRLS prowling the place.

After a few sips of his drink.

> DANIEL
> It's good to be back in Kuwait.
> It's good to see you again, it's
> been awhile.

The businessman doesn't answer.

> DANIEL (CONT'D)
> I need a favor.

> KUWAITI BUSINESSMAN
> Why should I help you?

> DANIEL
> Because we're friends.

> KUWAITI BUSINESSMAN
> You say we are friends. How come
> you only call me when you need help?
> But when I need something - you are
> too busy to pick up the phone. I
> don't think we are friends.

> DANIEL
> Fair enough. How about a V10
> Lamborghini? How's that for
> friendship?

EXT. LAMBORGHINI DEALERSHIP - KUWAIT CITY - NIGHT

They wait while a Lamborghini SALESMAN, disheveled, clearly just awakened, unlocks the door of the dealership.

                    DANIEL
               (to the Kuwaiti
               Businessman)
          The poor fucker had to get out of
          bed.
               (to the Salesman)
          As-salamu alaykum. Thanks my friend.

INT. LAMBORGHINI DEALERSHIP

They step inside and the salesman flicks on the lights revealing shiny cars displayed like jewels on rotating platforms. While the Kuwaiti businessman peers inside a silver model, Daniel confers with the salesman like he's bought twenty of these cars.

                    DANIEL
          Is this a Balboni? Fuck me. This
          is nice. What are you thinking?

                    KUWAITI BUSINESSMAN
          I think I'll choose this one.

The salesman retreats to a back office.

                    DANIEL
          That's a nice choice, my friend.

Daniel gives the Kuwaiti a slip of paper.

                    KUWAITI MAN
          Who is it?

                    DANIEL
          Who do you think? The guy's a
          terrorist. His mother lives here.
          I just need her phone number.

                    KUWAITI MAN
          There will be no repercussions in
          Kuwait?

                    DANIEL
          Somebody might die at some point in
          Pakistan.

They shake hands.

                                        CUT TO:

INT. SERVER ROOM - DAY

SUPERIMPOSE: TRADECRAFT

Sound graphs of phone calls fill the screen. We cruise through rows upon rows of server facilities, a single monitor in front traces a call to Rawalpindi, Pakistan.

                                                    CUT TO:

EXT. ISLAMABAD EMBASSY - THIRD STORY BALCONY - DAY

Maya chews on a peanut butter & jelly sandwich. Jack calls her on her cell.

                         MAYA
              Hey, Jack.

                         JACK
              You're not gonna like this, he's on
              the phone, but there's no team to
              deploy right now.

                         MAYA
              Fuck.

She dashes out runs down the hall to an Exit sign - bursts through the door to a staircase -

INT. EMBASSY STAIRCASE

- Flies down the staircase - down to another floor, barges through the door -

INT. AMERICAN EMBASSY CIA SECTION - SECURITY BAY - DAY

The station's surveillance team leader, LARRY, unstraps his flack vest. He looks like the kind of guy you don't mess with....so of course Maya barges into his space like a locomotive.

                         MAYA
              How come you haven't deployed a team
              to stay in Rawalpindi?

                         LARRY
              For one thing, it's dangerous. For
              another, the area is too congested
              for us to be effective without some
              predictive intelligence.

                         MAYA
              That's why you should forward deploy -
              so you can shorten your response
              time.

                         LARRY
              Still, it wouldn't work.

                         MAYA
              Why?

                    LARRY
The guy never stays on the phone
long enough.

                    MAYA
You haven't tried.

                    LARRY
Look, I don't have the personnel.

                    MAYA
That's bullshit.

                    LARRY
As it is, my guys don't get any sleep
tracking the threats within Pakistan.

Larry pushes past her to leave, and she follows him.

                    MAYA
Right, I understand. But I don't
really care if your guys get sleep
or not.

Maya looks at Larry's team sleeping on the couch.

INT. AMERICAN EMBASSY AMERICAN BAR - LATER

The conversation continues in the bar, for Maya has not
relented, although the tone is softer now. She offers Larry
a beer. He takes it.

                    LARRY
This guy you're obsessed with, what's
his name again?

                    MAYA
Abu Ahmed al Kuwaiti is the nom de
guerre. His true name, we think, is
Ibraheem Sayeed. His family lives
in Kuwait.

                    LARRY
Wasn't it, like, eight brothers -
and a million cousins - that we know
about - anyone could be calling home -

                    MAYA
I know -

                    LARRY
- It's not like he's saying, "Hey
mom, it's me, the terrorist."

                    MAYA
Over the course of two months, he's
called home from six different pay
phones, from two different cities,
                  (MORE)

                    MAYA (CONT'D)
          never using the same phone twice.
          And when his mother asked him where
          he was, he lied. He said that he
          was in a place in the country with
          bad cell reception -- implying he
          was in the Tribals -- but he was in
          a market in Peshawar. I'm sorry,
          but that's not normal guy behavior.
          That's tradecraft.

                    LARRY
          Maybe he just doesn't like his mom?
               (pause)
          Look, if he talks about an operation,
          or refers to anything remotely fishy,
          I'll get on him. Okay?

                    MAYA
          No. Not okay. Look, Abu Ahmed is
          too smart to tip his hand by talking
          about ops on the phone: <u>he works for</u>
          <u>bin Laden.</u> The guys that talk about
          ops on the phone don't get that job.

Larry looks away.

                    MAYA (CONT'D)
          A lot of my friends have died trying
          to do this.
               (pause)
          I believe I was spared so I could
          finish the job.

The girl is a true believer - as pure as they come.

Larry looks at her. Her sincerity is persuasive. And just
like that, he decides to help her.

                                        CUT TO:

INT. KOTLI CALL CENTER - RAWALPINDI, PAKISTAN

Hakim walks through a crowded call center. Larry joins him
from a back entrance. They look around: nothing.

EXT. RAWAL CALL CENTER - PAKISTAN

Hakim parks in front of the Rawal Call Center.

INT. RAWAL CALL CENTER - PAKISTAN - ANOTHER DAY

The call center is arranged into two rows of cubby-holes,
each separated by a privacy wall. Hakim searches the place,
finds nothing.

                                        CUT TO:

CU TV SCREEN: News reports of the attemped NYC bombing.

REPORTER (O.S.)
It is in surveillance video and
pictures like this of the explosive-
laden vehicle just moments before it
was parked, that police hope to find
the man who wanted so badly last
night to leave a body count in Times
Square.

CUT TO:

INT. AMERICAN EMBASSY CIA SECTION CUBICLE HALLWAY

The TV news report continues playing in the bg.

Bradley is moving as fast down a hallway. Coming towards
him like a shark from the other end of the hallway: Maya.

Bradley looks determined not to deal with her right now, and
lowers his head, but she spreads her arms slightly and
basically blocks his passage through the hallway

MAYA
I really need to talk to you about
beefing up our surveillance operation
on the caller.

BRADLEY
We don't have a surveillance operation
on the caller.
(turning to Maya)
Someone just tried to blow up Times
Square and you're talking to me about
some facilitator who some detainee
seven years ago said might have been
working with Al Qaeda?

Maya is practically shaking with zealous rage at her inability
to bend Bradley to her will.

MAYA
He's the key to bin Laden.

BRADLEY
I don't fucking care about bin Laden.
<u>I care about the next attack.</u> You're
going to start working on American
Al Qaeda cells. Protect the homeland.

MAYA
bin Laden is the one who keeps telling
them to attack the homeland. If it
wasn't for him, Al Qaeda would still
be focused on overseas targets. If
you really want to protect the
homeland, you need to get bin Laden.

                    BRADLEY
              (angry)
         This guy never met bin Laden.
         This guy is a free lancer working
         off the fucking internet. No one
         has even talked to bin Laden in four
         years: he's out of the game, he may
         well even be dead but you know what
         you're doing? You're chasing a ghost
         while the whole fucking network grows
         all around you!

For a moment she is silenced by Bradley's reprimand but then
Maya's obsession speaks for her - and like a woman possessed
she recklessly goes at him:

                    MAYA
         You just want me to nail some low
         level Mullah-crack-a-dulla so that
         you can check that box on your resume
         that says while you were in Pakistan
         you got a real terrorist. But the
         truth is you don't understand
         Pakistan, and you don't know Al Qaeda.
         Either give me the team I need to
         follow this lead, or the other thing
         you're gonna have on your resume is
         being the first Station Chief to be
         called before a congressional
         committee for subverting the efforts
         to capture or kill bin Laden.

                    BRADLEY
         You're fucking out of your mind.

                    MAYA
         I need four techs in a safe house in
         Rawalpindi and four techs in a safe
         house in Peshawar. Either send them
         out or send me back to DC and explain
         to the Director why you did it.

                                                  CUT TO:

INT. AMERICAN EMBASSY AMERICAN BAR - NIGHT

Maya, despondent, sits at the bar, drinking a beer.

Jack approaches.

                    JACK
         Fuck the mom, we got the man himself.

Jack puts a cell phone down on the counter.

                    JACK (CONT'D)
          Yesterday your caller bought himself
          a cell phone. And every time his
          phone rings -
                (he taps the cell
                phone)
          - *This* phone will ring. Did I hook
          you up?

Maya throws her arms around him.

                    MAYA
          I love you!

                                        CUT TO:

EXT. RAWALPINDI - ROAD - DAY

Larry drives his team around the narrow streets of Rawalpindi.
In the backseat, the COMPUTER TECH studies his laptop-like
tracking device.

                    MAYA O.S.
          My guess is that he lives close to
          where he's making the calls, and it
          makes sense he'd be living in
          Rawalpindi because there's an Al
          Jezerra office there.

INT. AMERICAN EMBASSY CIA SECTION - BRIEFING ROOM

We focus on a MAP of Pakistan on the wall. Maya is indicating
neighborhoods in Rawalpindi. She's briefing Bradley, Hakim,
Larry and a few other people.

                    MAYA
          It would be convenient for him to
          drop tapes off if he's sending either
          from bin Laden or from an
          intermediary. When he wants to make
          a call, he leaves the house, walks a
          few blocks, then switches on the
          phone. We need to keep canvassing
          the neighborhood until we find him.

EXT. STREETS OF RAWALPINDI / MINIVAN - CONTINUOUS

Larry is at the wheel, moving slowly through a dangerous
part of town. The streets narrow.

Two motorcycles suddenly pull around in front of Larry's van
and stop. The riders pull out guns.

INT. MINIVAN - CONTINUOUS

                    LARRY
          We got a shooter!

Larry tries reversing but a compact car wheels in right behind them, and Larry slams on the brakes. The TECH raises an M4.

>   TECH
>   We're blocked.

>   HAKIM
>   Let me talk to them.

EXT. STREETS OF RAWALPINDI

Hakim gets out of the car and walks toward the men. We can't hear what they're saying. At last, Hakim comes back to the car.

INT. MINIVAN

>   HAKIM
>   They said white faces don't belong
>   here. If they don't move, shoot
>   them.

A tense beat while the men stare, then finally leave.

INT. U.S. EMBASSY - ISLAMABAD - CUBICLE MAZE - DAY

On a large wall map, Maya circles "Peshawar" in red.

>   CUT TO:

EXT. ROADS/HIGHWAY - PAKISTAN

Larry's SUV speeds onto a highway, weaving in and out of dense traffic.

SUPERIMPOSE: PESHAWAR, PAKISTAN

INT. SUV

In the backseat, the Computer Tech is getting tossed around, trying to hang onto the Geo Locating device in his lap. The Geo Locator starts to BEEP - a blinking red light.

>   COMPUTER TECH
>   He's east of us. Try the market.

EXT./INT. MINIVAN

The congestion thickens. They slow to a crawl.

The SUV, stuck in traffic. Can't move.

Larry leaps out of the car and heads into an open air market -

EXT. OPEN AIR MARKET - PESHAWAR - CONTINUOUS

It's packed. All MEN - most with traditional beards worn by Al Qaeda members - many talking on cell phones.

Impossible to tell who is who. Impossible to find this needle in a haystack.

                                                    CUT TO:

EXT. MARKET - LATE AFTERNOON - ANOTHER DAY

The search continues... Hakim prowls a back alley. Then goes up on a rooftop to survey the activity below.

EXT. STREETS - TIPU ROAD - LATER

Hakim is on a street corner conducting surveillance. We follow him into a crowd and then lose sight...

We find him again, another street, another fruitless search.

As Hakim goes from street to street, we hear:

                    JACK O.S.
          We got a signal on Tipu Road for ten
          minutes. Then he went to Umar Road
          for five minutes. Nogaza Road.
          Darya Abad. That's in the Umar Road
          area. In Rawalpindi: Haider Road,
          Roomi Road. He went to the Convoy
          Road, which is near the hospital.
          So that's Haider, Roomi Road, Said,
          No Gaza, Taimur. He made a call
          from Haifa Street, that's the spice
          district.

                                                    CUT TO:

INT. U.S. EMBASSY - ISLAMABAD - MAYA'S DESK

Jack and Maya click through the tracking maps on her computer screen.

                    JACK
          Lahore street, which is also in Pesh,
          thirty minutes. Wazir Bag Road,
          five. Nishterabad, five. Phandu
          Road, five minutes, the Grand Trunk
          Road, forty five seconds. There's
          no pattern. Sometimes he calls every
          two weeks - sometimes every three -
          there's no consistency - I can't
          predict when he's gonna make another
          call because the guy's erratic.

                    MAYA
          Do you think its intentional?

                    JACK
          It might be. Maybe it just looks
          erratic to us. I just can't tell.

INT. MAYA'S APARTMENT - ISLAMABAD

Wearing a black burkha, Maya walks into her house and sinks
into the couch. She pulls off the head covering but doesn't
bother to remove the burkha. She switches on the TV. If
you didn't know her better, you'd think she'd gone native.

EXT. AMERICAN EMBASSY STREET - ISLAMABAD

Find Maya driving up to a check point mobbed with PROTESTERS
carrying signs - Joseph Bradley IS A CIA SPY! KILL THE SPY!
Bradley is CIA, etc.

>   REPORTER (O.S.)
>   Meanwhile, our chief foreign
>   correspondent, Richard Engel, confirms
>   the CIA's top spy in Pakistan has
>   been pulled out of there.

INT. MAYA'S CAR

The PROTESTERS have blocked the embassy check point. It's
going to take a long time to get through.

>   REPORTER (O.S.)
>   He's been receiving death threats
>   after being named publicly in a
>   lawsuit by the family of a victim of
>   a U.S. drone attack.

EXT. MAYA'S CAR

Several protesters notice her - they move to her car and
start banging on it.

                                                   CUT TO:

INT. AMERICAN EMBASSY CIA SECTION - STATION CHIEF'S OFFICE -
LATER

Maya and Bradley and several other STAFFERS watch the protest
through a window -

EXT. AMERICAN EMBASSY STREET

The CROWD grows larger and more unruly.

INT. STATION CHIEF'S OFFICE

>   MAYA
>   ISI fucked you. I'm so sorry Joseph.

It's the first time she's addressed him by his first name.
Startling, to hear kindness in her voice.

Joseph turns to reply then thinks better of it and walks
away.

                                                   CUT TO:

INT./ EXT LARRY'S MINIVAN - STREETS OF PESHAWAR - MORNING

Larry's minivan chugs through the crowded markets.

>   TECH
>   Still on tower three! Five. Signal
>   getting stronger. Ten!

Larry continues driving straight down the main road.

>   TECH (CONT'D)
>   Fifteen. Ten. Signal's getting
>   weaker.
>   (pause)
>   We lost him - no signal.

>   LARRY
>   Heading South.

The van passes horse-drawn carts, men on cell phones, fruit
stands. The Tech studies his screen.

>   TECH
>   He's up at five again. Fifteen.
>   Twenty.
>   (pause)
>   Weaker now, he's shifted. We're
>   back to five. I don't get it.

>   LARRY
>   He's driving in circles.

Larry now drives very fast back to the main road.

>   LARRY (CONT'D)
>   No change?

>   TECH
>   No.

MAIN ROAD

And now Larry stops in the middle of the market.

>   LARRY
>   Let's hope he comes back around.

Beat.

>   TECH
>   Twenty. Thirty. Forty! Fifty -
>   we're within ten meters of him.

Larry scans the street - sees a half dozen guys on cell
phones.

>   TECH (CONT'D)
>   He's really close.

                    LARRY
          Look at the cars. He's in a vehicle.

Larry spots something:

                    LARRY (CONT'D)
          The guy with the phone in the white
          SUV.

They snap a photograph of a WHITE POTAHAR SUV.

                    LARRY (CONT'D)
          Is that him?

                    TECH
          Could be.

                    LARRY
          You got him?

                    TECH
          I got him.

                    LARRY
          I'm breaking off -

The grey minivan pulls away.

                                        CUT TO:

INT. AMERICAN EMBASSY CIA SECTION - MAYA'S CUBICLE - DAY

Larry's photograph of the WHITE POTAHAR SUV plops on Maya's
desk.

                    MAYA
          Is this what I think it is?

                    LARRY
          The guy you've been looking for, geo-
          located on his cell phone in his
          white car.

                    MAYA
          Thank you!

                    LARRY
          If you're right, the whole world's
          gonna want in on this, so you gotta
          stick to your guns now.

                                        CUT TO:

INT. AMERICAN EMBASSY CIA SECTION - STATION CHIEF'S OFFICE

The new Chief of Station, TIM ALEXANDER, barely looks up
from his desk as Maya enters.

                        ALEXANDER
                  (into phone)
            I'm amazed that you're still here.
                  (looks at his watch,
                   into phone)
            When can we grab lunch?

He sees that Maya, who hovers annoyingly over his desk, isn't
gonna wait.

                        MAYA
            I need a picket line along the GT
            highway and men spaced at intervals
            along the road and at every exit.

                        ALEXANDER
            Maya, I know -

                        MAYA
            So you agree with me now. This is
            important?

                        ALEXANDER
            No, I've just learned from my
            predecessor that life is better when
            I don't disagree with you.

                                                  CUT TO:

EXT. GRAND TRUNK ROAD - PAKISTAN - DAY

A two lane highway. Tucked on the side of the road is an
OLD MAN with a cart of mangoes.

                        MAYA (V.O.)
            Our current hypothesis is that he
            lives somewhere along the highway,
            in one of the towns, or a medium
            sized city called Abbottabod, or up
            near Kashmir.

ECU: mango cart. Nestled among the fruit is a BLACK RADIO.

EXT. FARTHER DOWN GRAND TRUCK ROAD/HIGHWAY - CONTINUOUS

Squatting in the dirt near a bus stop is another OLD MAN,
watching passengers disembark from a bus.

                        MAYA (V.O.)
            Kashmir is interesting because it's
            a way station for the Tribals.

We stay with the old man for a while.

At last, the white POTAHAR SUV drives past. He makes a note
in his pad.

                                                  CUT TO:

EXT. HIGHWAY - MAJOR EXIT - DAY

A nut seller, another CIA look out, scoops a handful of nuts
into a bag for a CUSTOMER as he keeps an eye on CARS exiting
the highway.

He takes note as the white POTAHAR passes him.

                    MAYA (V.O.)
          Abbottabod is interesting because we
          know from detainee reporting that
          Faraj stayed there, briefly in 2003.

                                        CUT TO:

EXT. PAKISTANI STREET - DAY

The street is filled with compact cars.

                    MAYA (V.O.)
          The good news is he's driving a white
          SUV. SUV's are actually pretty rare
          in Pakistan. If he was driving a
          sedan or a compact, we'd be fucked.

                                        CUT TO:

INT. AMERICAN EMBASSY CIA SECTION - MAYA'S CUBICLE - NIGHT

                    MAYA (V.O.)
          Obviously this assumes he doesn't
          change vehicles.

Maya at her desk working and we realize that she has been
typing all this in a cable she will email to Washington.

                                        CUT TO:

EXT. MAYA'S APARTMENT BUILDING - ISLAMABAD - PRE DAWN

The building GUARD sees Maya heading out to her car.

                    GUARD
          Good morning.

                    MAYA
          Good morning, Amad.

Maya gets in her car. The gate opens. As she starts pulling
out onto the street, suddenly a car drives up in front of
her and THREE SHOOTERS come out and hammer Maya's Toyota.

INT. MAYA'S CAR - CONTINUOUS

- Bullets spider webbing the glass as Maya slams the car
into reverse -

EXT. MAYA'S CAR - CONTINUOUS

- Maya's guard starts returning fire, but his aim is terrible.

- SHOOTERS bear down on Maya, pumping bullets into her armored car. The gate closes, saving her, at the last possible moment.

INT. MAYA'S CAR - CONTINUOUS

Maya shakes inside her vehicle.

                    MAYA (PRE-LAP)
              (protesting)
      Any American in Pakistan is a target,
      they don't necessarily know I'm CIA.

                                        CUT TO

INT. AMERICAN EMBASSY STATION CHIEF'S OFFICE - ISLAMABAD - MORNING

                    ALEXANDER
      Doesn't matter. You're on a list.
      Next time there might not be
      bulletproof glass to save you.

                    MAYA
      Yeah.

                    ALEXANDER
      And you, of all people, should know
      that once you are on their list, you
      never get off.
              (pause)
      We'll keep up on the surveillance,
      as best we can.

                                        CUT TO:

EXT. RESIDENTIAL NEIGHBORHOOD - ABBOTTABAD, PAKISTAN - DAY

Hakim paces on a street as the POTAHAR we've been following drives past him. Hakim watches the vehicle enter a gated COMPOUND.

                                        CUT TO:

INT. CIA HEADQUARTERS PREDATOR BAY - LANGLEY - EVENING

The Langley Predator Bay is an impressive sight, a command center bristling with high-tech equipment. The room is filled with TECHNICIANS. George is in the center, where he belongs, directing traffic. People come up and give him new pieces of information.

The big screen displays a single image:

The overhead satellite image of the compound in Abbottabod.

SUPERIMPOSE: PREDATOR BAY - CIA HEADQUARTERS

From the back of the room, Maya enters, and watches the activity unfold without her... without her input.

George notices her, gives a thumbs up and then turns back to his troops.

STEVE, early 40s, a senior manager and one of George's top deputies, joins Maya.

> STEVE
> Basically we had a guy who rolled
> with Al Qaeda and did services for
> them. We lost him for seven years
> and now we found him again -- *and
> boy does he have a really nice house.*
> Is that it?

> MAYA
> Pretty much.

> STEVE
> Okay, let's go talk to the boss.

                                            CUT TO:

INT. LANGLEY BRIEFING ROOM

Maya and Steve are the first to arrive in the wood panelled conference room.

A detailed TABLE TOP MODEL of the compound sits in the center of the conference table, right next to a poster-sized satellite image of the compound.

She starts to sit in one of the chairs.

> STEVE
> (gentle)
> You should sit back there...sorry.

Steve points her to the back of the room.

> STEVE (CONT'D)
> They're gonna ask: if bin Laden is
> at the end of this rainbow - is the
> Pak military with him?

> MAYA
> The question isn't are the Paks
> protecting bin Laden?' The question
> is, 'would he allow himself to be
> protected by the Paks?'   I mean,
> why would he trust them? He tried
> to kill Musharaf.

Steve considers a reply, but the meeting principals are filing in, including Daniel, and when Steve sees the CIA DIRECTOR enter the room, he clears the head of the table.

>   CIA DIRECTOR
>   Go ahead.

>   STEVE
>   If you take a right out of Islamabad
>   and drive about forty-five minutes
>   North, you'll find yourself here in
>   Abbottabad. A middle class community -
>   some ex-military - not particularly
>   interesting to us. Except we did
>   find this compound, which is unique.
>   We got a sixteen foot wall around
>   the entire perimeter, the windows
>   are blacked out. It's a fortress.

>   CIA DIRECTOR
>   Can't you put a camera somewhere -
>   in the trees - to get a look into
>   the main house?

>   GEORGE
>   It will probably be discovered.

>   CIA DIRECTOR
>   We have to get a look into the house.

The Director moves to the satellite image.

>   CIA DIRECTOR (CONT'D)
>   Alright, what's this? This cluster
>   of buildings down here.

>   GEORGE
>   The PMA - The Pakistan Military
>   Academy. It's their West Point.

>   CIA DIRECTOR
>   And how close is that to the house?

>   GEORGE
>   About a mile.

A WOMAN'S voice from the back of the room.

>   MAYA O.S.
>   4,221 feet. It's closer to eight-
>   tenths of a mile.

>   CIA DIRECTOR
>   Who are you?

>   MAYA
>   I'm the motherfucker that found this
>   place, Sir.

The boss studies her for a moment then turns back to the
model.

> CIA DIRECTOR
> I want to know more about who's inside
> this house by the end of the week.

The brass files out, leaving Steve and Maya.

> STEVE
> "Motherfucker?" Really?

CUT TO:

INT. CIA HEADQUARTERS - AF/PAK DIVISION - DAY

Maya sits at her desk, frustrated, then walks down the aisle
of cubicles to the glass wall of George's office. She grabs
a red marker.

> MAYA
> (through the glass)
> Morning, George.

In red magic marker, Maya writes the number **21** on the glass.
Then circles it.

George looks up.

> MAYA (CONT'D)
> Twenty-one days. It's been twenty-
> one days since we found the house
> and nothing's happened!

INT. CIA HEADQUARTERS - PREDATOR BAY - NIGHT

We see a drone-fed overhead IMAGE of the bin Laden house in
real time with a resolution of 100 feet. Maya stares at the
screen, trying to decipher the shapes moving beneath her,
thousands of miles away.

The BLIPS move in increments, shadows lengthen.

CUT TO:

INT. CIA HEADQUARTERS - AF/PAK DIVISION - DAY

ECU - Maya erases the "51" on George's wall and replaces it
with "52."

George looks away.

INT. CIA HEADQUARTERS MAYA'S DESK - LATER

Maya sits at her desk. Her phone rings.

> MAYA
> (into phone)
> Yeah?

INT. CIA HEADQUARTERS - PREDATOR BAY

STEVE stares at drone image of the COMPOUND, which is under the joystick control of an IMAGERY TECHNICIAN.

>   STEVE
>   Swing by, I want to show you
>   something.

INT. CIA HEADQUARTERS MAYA'S DESK

Maya jumps up from her desk.

INT. CIA HEADQUARTERS - PREDATOR BAY - MOMENTS LATER

Maya walks in. Steve shows her images on the large monitor.

>   STEVE
>   This is from a few minutes ago. We've
>   got two males, two females, and seven
>   kids.

Maya points to one of the shapes in the courtyard.

>   MAYA
>   Who's that?

>   STEVE
>   I'm saying that's Bushra. The
>   brother's wife.

>   MAYA
>   How do you know the gender?

>   STEVE
>   (points on screen, to
>   a thin line)
>   This is a clothes-line here, for
>   laundry. Men don't mess with the
>   wash.

We watch that shape move away from the clothes-line and back to the house.

>   STEVE (CONT'D)
>   It takes her about four seconds to
>   move from there to the front door.
>   So she's on the older side.

>   MAYA
>   What's that up there?
>   (pointing to the other
>   shapes)

>   STEVE
>   Those are kids. They're shuffling
>   around, sword-fighting or something
>   with sticks.
>   (MORE)

                    STEVE (CONT'D)
          (pointing again)
     You can see their height relative to
     this - these are cows - so they're
     probably between seven and nine.
     Boys.

Another FIGURE comes out of the house and moves to the clothes-
line and grabs some laundry.

                    MAYA
     Your female is moving fast.

                    STEVE
     That's what I wanted to show you.
          (to the Imagery
           Technician)
     Can we pause this please?
          (to Maya)
     That's not the same lady. That's
     female #3.

                    MAYA
     So you found two males, three females?

                    STEVE
     That's correct.

Maya suddenly gets it.

                    MAYA
     You're missing a male.

                    STEVE
     Yes we are.

                    MAYA
     Wow.

INT. WHITE HOUSE - NATIONAL SECURITY COUNCIL S.C.I.F. -
CONTINUOUS

George is on one side of a conference table, on the other
side is the DEPUTY NATIONAL SECURITY ADVISOR, THE SPECIAL
ASSISTANT TO THE DEPUTY NATIONAL SECURITY ADVISOR, and the
NATIONAL SECURITY ADVISOR.

                    GEORGE
     If there are three females, there
     ought to be *three males*. Observant
     Muslim women either live with parents
     or with their husbands. We think
     there's a third family living in the
     house.

SUPERIMPOSE: SITUATION ROOM - THE WHITE HOUSE

                    NATIONAL SECURITY ADVISOR
          So this third male that you've
          identified as possibly being bin
          Laden, do I just give up all hope of
          ever seeing a photograph of him?

                    GEORGE
          Hope? Hope is not a targeting layer.
          You give up your hope right now. We
          scanned for heat signatures, but we
          can't validate if it's a man or a
          woman up there. We found a safe
          house, but we can't get a vantage
          point to fire a telescope over the
          balcony wall.

EXT. COMPOUND - ABBOTTABAD - MORNING

A DOCTOR comes to the compound offering immunizations. One
of the women let's him in, and he offers polio vaccines to
the children.

                    GEORGE
          We talked about burrowing a pin hole
          camera but there's a high risk of
          discovery. We have explored the
          possibility of digging tunnels, of
          sending hot air balloons, of re-
          routing supply C-130's to take a
          peek, but that might be too alerting.
          We've looked for ways of collecting
          available DNA from his trash - you
          know, looking for his toothbrush,
          but they burn the trash. We started
          a vaccination program, we sent a
          doctor to the house, to see if he
          could pull blood.

A lady in a black burkha rushes out and angrily shoos the
doctor away.

                    GEORGE (CONT'D)
          That didn't work out. We thought
          about sending a guy with a bucket to
          pull a sample from the sewer to
          analyze his fecal matter.

                    SPECIAL ASSISTANT TO THE ADVISOR
          What was wrong with that, exactly?

He looks up.

                    GEORGE
          What was wrong with that? The sample
          would be too diluted.

                    NATIONAL SECURITY ADVISOR
And it's asking too much to get a
voice confirmation with him on the
phone?

                    GEORGE
They don't make telephone calls from
the compound. We pulled the cell
tower nearby.

                    NATIONAL SECURITY ADVISOR
And I'm also going to give up hope
that he might ever get in that white
SUV and drive around a bit and we
could see him? Don't they get
groceries.

                    GEORGE
The unidentified third male does not
get groceries. He does not leave
the compound. He does not present
himself for photographs. When he
needs fresh air, he paces around
beneath a grape arbor, but the leaves
are so thick they obscure our
satellite views. This is a
professional attempt to avoid
detection - real tradecraft. The
only people we've seen behave this
way are other top level Al Qaeda
operatives.

The National Security Advisor nods to his Special Assistant
who slides a big folder across his desk to George.

                    NATIONAL SECURITY ADVISOR
We did a Red Team on your analysis.
According to them, this behavior
could belong to someone other than
Al Qaeda.

                    DEPUTY NATIONAL SECURITY ADVISOR
They did give a forty percent chance
that the unidentified third man is a
senior Al Qaeda operative. But they
also said there's a thirty-five
percent chance he's a Saudi drug
dealer
          (reading from the
           binder)
A fifteen percent chance that he's a
Kuwaiti arms smuggler, a ten percent
chance that he's one of the relatives
of the brothers.

                    SPECIAL ASSISTANT TO THE ADVISOR
          Basically, we agree with you, the
          house screams security, it screams
          someone who wants privacy, it even
          screams 'bad guy', but it does not
          scream bin Laden.

                    NATIONAL SECURITY ADVISOR
          You get the point.
              (beat)
          If you can't prove it's bin Laden,
          at least prove it's not somebody
          else, like a drug dealer.

Beat.

The meeting is adjourned.

As they walk out --

                    GEORGE
          You know we lost our ability to prove
          that when we lost the detainee
          program.
              (beat)
          Who the hell am I supposed to ask?
          Some guy in Gitmo who is all lawyered
          up? He'll just tell his lawyer to
          warn bin Laden.

                    NATIONAL SECURITY ADVISOR
          You'll think of something.

                                             CUT TO:

INT. CIA HEADQUARTERS - AF/PAK DIVISION - DAY

Maya is back at George's office, keeping track of time for
us by writing each passing day on the window of George's
office.

We watch as she erases the numbers in red and writes new
ones. **78.**

Time passes.

98. 99. 100.

100 days. She underscores the numerals in thick magic marker.

                                             CUT TO:

INT. WHITE HOUSE - NATIONAL SECURITY COUNCIL S.C.I.F. - DAY

The same group around the same conference table.

> GEORGE
> He'd be the first successful drug
> dealer never to have dealt drugs.
> He has no internet access to the
> house. He makes no phone calls either
> in or out. Who's he selling to,
> who's he buying from, how's he making
> his money? And if you're going to
> say he's retired, I'd say where's
> his swimming pool, where's the gold
> cage with the falcons? And why does
> he send his courier to the two cities
> in Pakistan we most associate with
> Al Qaeda, that have nothing
> particularly to do with heroin
> production?

The National Security Advisor taps his pencil impatiently.

> NATIONAL SECURITY ADVISOR
> The President is a thoughtful,
> analytical guy. He needs proof.

                                                        CUT TO:

INT. WHITE HOUSE HALLWAY

The National Security Advisor and his team file out. George
approaches.

> GEORGE
> I have to admit, I just don't get
> the rhythms of politics.

> NATIONAL SECURITY ADVISOR
> You think this is political? If
> this was political we'd be having
> this conversation in October when
> there's an election bump. This is
> pure risk. Based on deductive
> reasoning, inference, supposition
> and the only human reporting you
> have is six years old, from detainees
> who are questioned under duress.
> The political move here is to tell
> you to go fuck yourself, and remind
> you that I was in the room when your
> old boss pitched WMD Iraq...at least
> there you guys brought photographs.

> GEORGE
> You know, you're right, I agree with
> everything you just said. What I
> meant was, a man in your position,
> how do you evaluate the risk of *not*
> doing something, the risk of
> potentially letting bin Laden slip
> through your fingers?

George shakes his head with an "aww shucks" kind of shake.

                    GEORGE (CONT'D)
          That is a fascinating question.

George walks away. After a beat, the National Security
advisor calls after him.

               NATIONAL SECURITY ADVISOR
          Hey.

George turns around. The National Security Advisor approaches
him.

          NATIONAL SECURITY ADVISOR (CONT'D)
               (lowering his voice)
          I'm not saying we're gonna do it.
          But the President wants to know: if
          we were going to act, how would we
          do it? Give us options.

                                        CUT TO:

EXT. AIR FORCE BASE - AIRPLANE HANGAR - DAY

SUPERIMPOSE: AREA 51 - SOUTHERN NEVADA

Doors of a HANGAR open in front of a large crowd that includes
several White House guys, a General, and a squadron of Navy
SEALs, including PATRICK, JUSTIN, JARED, SABER, TWO SOAR
PILOTS, and some members of the Af-Pak department, George,
Daniel, Hakim, and of course, Maya. The doors grind open to
reveal: TWO STEALTH BLACKHAWKS

                    GENERAL
          I actually tried to kill this program
          a couple of times. They've gone
          through an initial round of testing,
          and they have excellent radar defeat -
          we just haven't tested them with
          people in them yet.

The General continues his briefing..

                    GENERAL (CONT'D)
          You'll notice these stealth panels
          similar to what we use on the B2 -
               (pointing to the rotors)
          - The rotors have been muffled with
          decibel killers - it's slower than a
          Blackhawk and lacks the offense.
          But it can hide.

                    JUSTIN
          Excuse me. Can I ask a question?
          What do we need this for in Libya?
          Gaddafi's anti-air is virtually non-
          existent.

Maya looks over, not sure what to say.

                    GEORGE
          Gentlemen, can I have your attention?
          My name is George. I run the Af-Pak
          division at CTC, and I'm primary on
          this for the agency. This is a title
          fifty operation. Some of us have
          worked together before. This is a
          good one. Maya, do you want to brief
          them?

Maya looks at the SEALs. Folds her arms. This isn't going
to be easy.

                    MAYA
          There are two narratives about the
          location of Osama bin Laden.

This registers on the SEALs.

                    MAYA (CONT'D)
          The one that you're most familiar
          with is that UBL is hiding in a cave
          in the Tribal Areas, that he's
          surrounded by a large contingent of
          loyal fighters.

Beat.

                    MAYA (CONT'D)
          But that narrative is pre- 9/11
          understanding of UBL.
          The second narrative is that he's
          living in a city - living in a city
          with multiple points of egress and
          entries and with access to
          communications so that he can keep
          in touch with the organization. You
          can't run a global network of inter-
          connected cells from a cave.

Beat.

                    MAYA (CONT'D)
          We've located an individual we believe
          based on detainee reporting is bin
          Laden's courier. He's living in a
          house in Abbottabod, Pakistan. And
          we assess that one of the other
          occupants of the house is UBL.

                    JUSTIN
          Excuse me. You got an intel source
          on the ground?

                    MAYA
          No.

                         JUSTIN
          No? Okay, so how do you know it's
          bin Laden? We've been on this op
          before, you know.

                         MAYA
          Bin Laden uses a courier to interact
          with the outside world. By locating
          the courier, we've located bin Laden.

                         PATRICK
          That's really the intel? That's it?

                         MAYA
          Quite frankly, I didn't even want to
          use you guys, with your dip and your
          velcro and all your gear bullshit.
          I wanted to drop a bomb but people
          didn't believe in this lead enough
          to drop a bomb, so they're using you
          guys as canaries on the theory that
          if bin Laden isn't there, you can
          sneak away and no one will be the
          wiser.
               (beat)
          But bin Laden is there - and you're
          going to kill him for me.

                         PATRICK
               (softening)
          Bullets are cheap.

                                             CUT TO:

INT. CIA HEADQUARTERS - GEORGE'S OFFICE - DAY

George is shaking his head as he talks to Wolf.

                         GEORGE
          They are nervous downtown. I don't
          think we'll get approval this decision
          cycle.

They look up and notice that Maya is standing outside George's
office staring at them through the glass.

She angrily wipes the number **128** off the window and changes
it to **129.**

Wolf nods.

                         WOLF
          It's her against the world.

                         GEORGE
          Oh yeah.

                                             CUT TO:

INT. CIA HEADQUARTERS - CAFETERIA - DAY

George is pulling his tray away from the food service court
when Maya ambushes him.

>   MAYA
>   We've spun up the SEALs - we've done
>   everything humanly possible to collect
>   on the compound, and the collection
>   is not going to get any better.

>   GEORGE
>   We have to keep working it.

>   MAYA
>   You're going to come into work one
>   day, and there's going to be a black
>   moving van and a 'for sale' sign in
>   front of that compound.

George drops his tray down.

>   GEORGE
>   Maya, you didn't prove it.

INT. CIA HEADQUARTERS - 7TH FLOOR - CONFERENCE ROOM - DAY

Sitting around the table are the CIA Director, JEREMY, Wolf,
the DEPUTY DIRECTOR, George, Daniel, Steve and a few other
people we don't know. At the far end of the table are back
benchers, including Maya.

>   CIA DIRECTOR
>   I'm about to go look the President
>   in the eye and what I'd like to know,
>   no fucking bullshit, is where everyone
>   stands on this thing. Now, very
>   simply. Is he there or is he not
>   fucking there?

He looks to the Deputy Director.

>   DEPUTY DIRECTOR
>   We all come at this through the filter
>   of our own past experiences. I
>   remember Iraq WMD very clearly, I
>   fronted that and I can tell you the
>   case for that was much stronger than
>   this case.

>   CIA DIRECTOR
>   Yes or no.

>   DEPUTY DIRECTOR
>   We don't deal in certainty, we deal
>   in probability. I'd say there's a
>   sixty percent probability he's there.

The CIA Director points to Wolf.

                    WOLF
          I concur. Sixty percent.

                    GEORGE
          I'm at eighty percent. Their OPSEC
          is what convinces me.

                    CIA DIRECTOR
          You guys ever agree on anything?

                    DANIEL
          Well, I agree with sixty, we're basing
          this mostly on detainee reporting
          and I spent a bunch of time in those
          rooms - who knows?

Maya shoots Daniel a look. What a traitor.

                    DANIEL (CONT'D)
          I'd say it's a soft sixty, sir. I'm
          virtually certain there's some high
          value target there, I'm just not
          sure it's bin Laden.

The CIA Director leans back in his chair.

                    CIA DIRECTOR
          This is a cluster-fuck, isn't it?

                    JEREMY
          I'd like to know what Maya thinks.

                    DEPUTY DIRECTOR
          We're all incorporating her assessment
          into ours.

Maya can't take it anymore:

                    MAYA
          One hundred percent, he's there -
          okay, fine, ninety-five percent
          because I know certainty freaks you
          guys out - but it's a hundred!

INT. CIA HEADQUARTERS - 7TH FLOOR - HALLWAY

The CIA Director walks with Jeremy towards the elevator.

                    CIA DIRECTOR
          They're all cowed. What do you think
          of the girl?

                    JEREMY
          I think she's fucking smart.

As the door closes.

                    CIA DIRECTOR
          We're all smart, Jeremy.

INT. LANGELY CAFETERIA

Maya is eating lunch by herself when she's startled to see
the CIA Director standing by her table.

                    CIA DIRECTOR
          May I join you?

She nods, gulps.

                    CIA DIRECTOR (CONT'D)
               (sitting)
          How long have you worked for the
          CIA?

                    MAYA
          Twelve years. I was recruited out
          of high school.

                    CIA DIRECTOR
          Do you know why we did that?

                    MAYA
          I don't think I can answer that
          question, sir. I don't think I'm
          allowed to answer.

                    CIA DIRECTOR
          What else have you done for us besides
          bin Laden?

                    MAYA
          Nothing. I've done nothing else.

He evaluates her... weighing her certainty against his decades
of Washington experience.

                    CIA DIRECTOR
          Well, you certainly have a flare for
          it.

                                        FADE TO BLACK:

SUPERIMPOSE: THE CANARIES

EXT. JALALABAD FORWARD OPERATING BASE - AFGHANISTAN - DAY

Jalalabad Airfield: nestled against the rugged mountains of
the Pakistan border.

SUPERIMPOSE: FORWARD OPERATING BASE - JALALABAD, AFGHANISTAN -
MAY 1, 2011

Everything in motion, SOLDIERS, CONTRACTORS, AVIATION ASSETS,
PATROLS coming and going.

EXT.   JALALABAD FORWARD OPERATING BASE - AFTERNOON

Patrick and Justin are playing horseshoes. Maya, happy for
the first time since we've met her, watches them

                    JUSTIN
          So, Patrick, be honest with me. You
          really believe this story?
               (to Maya)
          No offense.

                    PATRICK
          I do.

                    JUSTIN
          What part convinced you?

Patrick motions to Maya.

                    PATRICK
          Her confidence.

Maya smiles, laughs.

                    JUSTIN
          Really? Okay. That's the kind of
          concrete data point I'm looking for.

He shakes his head.

                    JUSTIN (CONT'D)
          If her confidence is the one thing
          that's keeping me from getting ass-
          raped in a Pakistani prison...I don't
          know. I'm gonna be honest with you
          though, I guess I'm cool with it.

They bump fists, laughing. Maya's cell phone rings. She
moves aside to answer it.

We INTERCUT with George in his Langley office.

                    GEORGE
          Maya, I wanted you to hear it first.
          You know that thing we talked about?
          It's going to happen.

                    MAYA
          When?

                    GEORGE
          Tonight. Good luck.

She hangs up, turns back to the SEALs, who are still playing
horseshoes with the grace of young guys in their prime.

Their lives are in her hands.

                                             CUT TO:

INT. ASSAULT COMMAND CENTER - JALALABAD FORWARD OPERATING
BASE - DAY

The small space is filled with personnel and
telecommunications gear. At the back of the room Maya sits
quietly, adjusting a headset and speaking calmly into a secure
line. From the corner Hakim watches her.

                    MAYA
          Testing - testing 1 - 2 - 3 -

A SEAL with his com set on gives her the thumbs up. She
looks around at all the impressive technology in the makeshift
Command Center. She walks over to Hakim and they leave
together.

EXT. JALALABAD FORWARD OPERATING BASE - DUSK

                    MAYA
          Thank you for coming with me.

                    HAKIM
          Of course. I'll go with you where
          ever you want.

A few hundred feet in front of them they can see SEALs
preparing their gear.

                    MAYA
          Fuck Hakim, what if I'm wrong? I
          wish we could have just dropped a
          bomb.

                    HAKIM
          Please don't drop it while we're in
          the house.

                    MAYA
          I'm serious.

                    HAKIM
          Me too. Don't drop anything while
          I'm inside.

Off her anxious smile --

                                              CUT TO:

EXT. FORWARD OPERATING BASE JALALABAD, AFGHANISTAN - OUTER
LZ - NIGHT

Blinding white lights - rigged to chain link fencing, like a
space shuttle launch -

Silhouetted shapes behind the lights and the thump-thump-
thump SOUND of high-dollar helicopters -

Now push through the glare and the fence into -

EXT. FORWARD OPERATING BASE JALALABAD, AFGHANISTAN - INNER
LZ

A top-secret LZ.

Where twenty-two SEALs in full battle rattle and an attack
DOG load into TWO STEALTH BLACKHAWK helicopters

Moving fast, wordlessly, loading weapons and gear - under
the intense bright white light, then -

- Doors slam, engines whine -

Fifty yards away, Maya stands alone, looking on.

- And the HELOS rise above the lights and disappear into the
night.

INT. STEALTH BLACKHAWK HELICOPTER - PRINCE 52 - PILOT'S CABIN

Hands feather the controls as the pilot -- one the famed
Nightstalker's from the Special Operations Aviation Regiment
(SOAR) 160th -- flies without lights, using only his NODs
for night vision.

EXT. STEALTH BLACKHAWK HELICOPTERS PRINCE 51 AND PRINCE 52

Flying in formation, barely visible in the moonless sky, no
flying lights.

The helos near the Tora Bora mountain range: dimly visible
bulks rising in front of the helos.

INT. PRINCE 51 - CABIN

The SEALs gently bounce inside the bellies of the churning
beasts.

                    PRINCE 51 PILOT
          Thirty seconds to first turn.

                    JARED
          Hey Justin, what are you listening
          to?

                    JUSTIN
          Tony Robbins.

                    JARED
          Tony Robbins?

                    JUSTIN
          You should listen to it. I got plans
          for after this. I want to talk to
          you guys about it. It's not selling.
          You become a representative.

Everyone chuckles.

                    PRINCE 51 CO-PILOT
          Hard left.

EXT. PRINCE 51 AND PRINCE 52 - FLYING IN FORMATION

The stealths take a sharp turn. Skimming the mountain.

                    PATRICK
          Who here's been in a helo crash
          before?

Everyone raises their hands.

                    PATRICK (CONT'D)
          Okay, so we're all good.

                                        CUT TO:

INT. ASSAULT COMMAND CENTER - JALALABAD FORWARD OPERATING
BASE - EVENING

Technicians track the helos on an array of computer screens.

                    PRINCE 52 PILOT
              (over radio)
          Now entering Pakistan.

Maya is here, too, working. She's always working.

                    MAYA
              (into headset)
          Pakistani coms, no chatter.

EXT. TORA BORA MOUNTAINS - LATER

Find the HELICOPTERS navigating tight mountain passes. NOTE:
Throughout the flying sequence that follows the helicopters
fly very close to the ground, with a margin of error less
then twenty feet.

                                        CUT TO:

PILOT POV:

The terrain zooms by as we travel through a twisty mountain
pass -

- Looming straight ahead on a collision course is a GIANT
MOUNTAIN. They zoom closer. We can see individual rocks now -

INT. PRINCE 51

                    PRINCE 51 PILOT
              (into radio)
          Big left!

STILLS

Jessica Chastain

Jason Clarke

Mark Boal and Jessica Chastain

Edgar Ramirez and Jessica Chastain

Kyle Chandler and Jessica Chastain

Jennifer Ehle

Fredric Lehne

Mark Strong

Stephen Dillane and Mark Strong

James Gandolfini

Kathryn Bigelow and Mark Boal

The film's recreation of the Abbottabad compound, built to exact detail.

EXT. TORA BORA MOUNTAINS

Seconds before impact, the HELICOPTERS bank into a hard left
turn.

DUST blows off the mountain.

CUT TO:

INT. PRINCE 51 - LATER

The dog PANTS - sitting in its handler's lap in the dim cabin -

                    PILOT
          Ten minutes.

CUT TO:

INT. PRINCE 51 - LATER

                    PILOT
          Three mikes to target. Standby for
          doors open.

Inside the dim interior, illuminated by only blinking
instrumentation, the men are tense, quiet.

We pass slowly from face to face, noting each SEAL's
contemplation of the mission that lies ahead.

Some of them are anonymous soldiers. Many we've come to
know: Justin, joyfully bobbing his head, grooving to his
iPod... Saber's eyes fixed on a thousand-yard stare... Hakim
struggles to get comfortable and control his anxiety, wipes
away sweat... Patrick checks his gear for the hundredth time.

                    CO-PILOT
          Two minutes.

EXT. STEALTH BLACKHAWKS - PRINCE 51 AND PRINCE 52 -

Outside: Darkness....just a THUMP THUMP THUMP....

And then we see them: flying in tight formation, the oddly
rectangular helos, with their black stealth panels and sharp
edges, like two alien spaceships advancing.

INT. EXT STEALTH BLACKHAWK - NIGHT

                    PILOT
                 (over intercom)
          Should be coming up just off our
          nose, 3 o'clock.

Everyone grabs onto their gear, getting ready to fast rope.

DOOR

Patrick flings open the side door. Night wind rushes in -

EXT. ABBOTTABAD, PAKISTAN - NIGHT

Small cottages mixed in with larger suburban homes. Among
them, swimming pools. The water shimmering. Surreal. Then:
rows of green fields. A stand of trees.

It appears: AC 1. It is massive - six or seven times larger
than any other nearby structure - with sixteen foot high
walls and a gated interior. A fortress.

INT. PRINCE 51 - CONTINUOUS

                    PILOT
          Thirty seconds.

Patrick leans out for a visual as the wind rips his face -

EXT. PRINCE 51 AND PRINCE 52

The helos circle the COMPOUND, kicking up dust, and begin to
descend.

INT./EXT. STEALTH BLACKHAWK HELICOPTER PRINCE 51 - NIGHT

Cross cutting all that follows:

- At thirty feet above the ground the helicopter begins to
shudder and lose stability. Instead of descending in a
straight path, the bird drifts sideways

                    PATRICK
              (shouting to pilot)
          Hey! Slide right.

- Then lurches down, falling to within 15 feet of the swirling
ground, rotors churning the dust, creating near BROWNOUT
conditions, a dust hurricane

INT. PRINCE 51

CU: Pilot finessing the controls - not good enough

                    PRINCE 51 PILOT
          Power!

EXT. COMPOUND - NIGHT

ECU: rear rotor blades edging closer to the wall, inch by
inch.

-- Engines straining LOUDLY in the thin, hot air

-- The bird loses control, SPINS to a hard landing

INT. PRINCE 51

ECU: Pilot thrusts stick

EXT. COMPOUND

-- TAIL crashes hard on the WALL, in a awful screech of twisting metal and sheared concrete -

INT. PRINCE 51

-- Tossing the men inside the helo around like rag dolls.

                                        CUT TO:

INT. ASSAULT COMMAND CENTER - JALALABAD FORWARD OPERATING BASE - EVENING

The command tent watches the helicopter crash.

                     PRINCE 52 PILOT   (O.S.)
                Prince 51 is down. Blackhawk down
                in the animal pen.

Maya stands, crestfallen.

EXT. HELO CRASH

The dust settles to reveal...a twisted wreck.

PRINCE 51 has crash landed into a precarious position, with the back half of the helicopter wedged into the top of the wall and the front of it in the ground, leaving the passengers inside suspended more then ten feet off the ground.

INT./EXT. PRINCE 51

Although he's wearing a heavy pack and carrying gear, Patrick jumps down, landing with a knee-shattering combat roll.

Several SEALs follow him.

EXT. INNER COURTYARD

Patrick pulls out of his roll and turns around to face the house, looming ominously ahead of him.

INT. ASSAULT COMMAND CENTER - JALALABAD FORWARD OPERATING BASE - EVENING

                     PRINCE 52 PILOT
                  (over radio)
                This mission is still a go.

Off Maya's relief -

INT./EXT. PRINCE 52 - CONTINUOUS

The second helo passes over but a storm of debris and garbage from the rooftop creates another flight risk and the helo banks away.

                                        CUT TO:

EXT. COMPOUND - FIRST GATE

Patrick, Justin and SIX other SEALs cluster near the First
Gate in the animal pen. One of the SEALs places a charge on
the gate, while others check the Prayer Room.

Boom! The charge partially blows open the metal swing doors
of the gate, leaving a very narrow gap. Not ideal. The
SEALs muscle and squeeze their way through the narrow opening
in the jagged metal as the SNIPER climbs up on the roof of
the prayer room.

EXT. GUEST HOUSE - NIGHT

Patrick and Jared arrive at the guest house but can't see
inside - the windows and doors are covered with sheets.
Patrick kneels down to place a charge at the front door handle
when the door erupts with gunfire

- Bullets fly out of the wooden door. One skims Patrick's
shoulder as he kneels lower. Patrick fires back at the house,
putting a dozen rounds inside.

A moment passes. They wait for a response. The door handle
unlocks. ABU AHMED'S WIFE appears at the doorway and walks
out.

                    JARED
          Ir-fah ee-dek!

                    ABU AHMED'S WIFE
               (in English)
          You killed him.

INT. GUEST HOUSE - CONTINUOUS

The SEALs peer inside and see ABU AHMED lying dead in a
pool of blood. Patrick and Jared pump safety rounds into
the body.

FOUR KIDS are cowering in the corner. Jared moves them out
of the house.

EXT. COMPOUND - DIEGO CORRIDOR - CONTINUOUS

The rest of the P51 SEALS breach a gate to the courtyard of
the Main House. The gate flies open in a fiery ball.

                                        CUT TO:

EXT. COMPOUND WALLS OUTSIDE MAIN GATE - CONTINUOUS

SEALs jump out of P52, rush to the outer wall and set
breaching charges on a gate... While Hakim, the DOG HANDLER,
and another SEAL peel off down the block

Saber and his team stand by as BOOM!!!, The gate charges go
off...only to reveal a BRICK WALL behind the gate.

                         SABER
            That's not a door.

                          SEAL
            Failed breach.

They hustle to the next entry way and prepare another breach

                                                  CUT TO:

EXT. MAIN HOUSE - COURTYARD

The COMMANDING OFFICER hears that the SEALs outside are
preparing a charge. SEAL MIKE radios in

                    SEAL MIKE (O.S.)
                (into radio)
            This is Echo 11, we're going to breach
            the main gate.

                    COMMANDING OFFICER
                (into radio)
            Negative. I'm internal, I'll let
            you in.

The Commanding Officer opens the gate and the other SEALs
walk inside. As a group, they move towards the main house,
arriving at the South side front door. The door is open and
they enter -

INT. MAIN HOUSE FIRST FLOOR - CONTINUOUS

Piercing the first floor darkness with their infra red lights,
the SEALs advance slowly into the first floor hallway.

Piles of household clutter, stacked high in bizarre shapes,
greet them like the innards of a haunted house. One of the
SEAL's catches movement: A figure with an AK-47 scrambling
through clutter, then disappearing around a corner.

                         JUSTIN
                Abrar!

The figure, Abu Ahmed's brother, ABRAR, re-appears at the
end of the hallway. He pokes his head out -

- And is shot by Justin. He falls out of view, whimpering
in pain.

INT. MAIN HOUSE - FIRST FLOOR HALLWAY - CONTINUOUS

Justin walks quickly to Abrar.

INT. MAIN HOUSE - FIRST FLOOR SIDE ROOM - CONTINUOUS

ABRAR is down, bleeding.

- Justin fires another round into Abrar as ABRAR'S WIFE comes flying in from the sleeping quarters and shields him with her body.

- Justin shoots her. She falls...Abrar is underneath her - he is still breathing, gasping and

- Justin shoots him again, silencing him

- Then looks to his wife and assesses her condition

- Badly wounded, faint breathing, life fading from her eyes...

- Justin turns away

INT. MAIN HOUSE - FIRST FLOOR HALLWAY - CONTINUOUS

Justin and a BREACHER proceed down the hall to the heavy gate that blocks access to the stairway while another SEAL stays behind. Somewhere, children are screaming.

                    JUSTIN
          Shut those fucking kids up.

O.S. the kids quiet down.

                    JUSTIN (CONT'D)
          Talk to me.

                    BREACHER
          There's no fucking way we want to
          blow this thing. The gate is solid.

                    MIKE   (O.S.)
              (over radio)
          This is Echo 11 - we're at our primary
          set point, prepping to breach.

                    JUSTIN
              (into radio)
          Wait, Echo 11 - we're internal on
          the south side - this is a negative
          breach.

                    MIKE
              (over radio)
          Roger. We're ready to make our entry
          out here.

                    JUSTIN
              (into radio)
          Roger that, we're coming to meet
          you.
              (to the Breacher)
          Stay with these kids. Don't let
          them in the back room.

                                                  CUT TO:

EXT. MAIN HOUSE - A MOMENT LATER

In the regrouping that occurs on the side of the main house, Justin and Patrick find themselves side by side - and the old friends take a moment to reconnect while the rest of the team places charges and prepares for the next phase of the assault.

                    PATRICK
          (quietly)
     You good?

                    JUSTIN
     Yeah. I forgot...were we supposed
     to crash that helo?

Patrick allows himself a smile.

                    PATRICK
     Ibrahim tried to shoot me through
     the door. I popped him from the
     outside.

                    JUSTIN
     I fucking smoked Abrar and his wife.
          (shifting tone)
          (alt: I think she was
           pregnant)

                    PATRICK
     Still alive?

                    JUSTIN
     She's gonna bleed out.

                    PATRICK
     What a fuckin' mess -

The door blows - and they keep moving -

INT. MAIN HOUSE - FIRST FLOOR HALLWAY - CONTINUOUS

The SEALs reach the staircase, which is sealed off by a separate metal gate than the one inside the hallway.

                    SEAL
     Breacher up.

A charge is prepared. Justin, who is now inside one of the side rooms, sees Jared standing close to the door.

                    JUSTIN
     Hey man, move!

Jared moves just as -

EXT. MAIN HOUSE FIRST FLOOR HALLWAY - CONTINUOUS

- Boooom!

-- The door FLIES like a missile right into where Jared had been standing.

                    JARED
              (to Justin)
          Thanks.

                    JUSTIN
          Yeah.

                                        CUT TO:

INT. MAIN HOUSE - STAIRCASE TO SECOND FLOOR - CONTINUOUS

Saber goes up the staircase, Patrick following closely behind him, climbing up to see -

INT. MAIN HOUSE - SECOND FLOOR - CONTINUOUS

A man ducks out of sight. Saber calls to him.

                    SABER
          Khaled!

Saber waits with his carbine raised. Anxiety crosses his face. He's vulnerable here, an easy target if Khaled were to come out blasting.

                    SABER (CONT'D)
          KHALED!

                                        CUT TO:

INT. SECOND FLOOR HALLWAY

Khaled hears his name being called from below. A few feet away from him in the dimly lit hall is a loaded AK-47. He goes to the gun and picks it up.

He hears his name again, "Khaled!" And the voice sounds friendly, urgent.

Perhaps thinking that he can surrender peacefully, Khaled puts the gun down, resting it against a wall, and turns and heads back to the sound of his name.

Saber sees Khaled poke his head around the corner of the stairway and fires - killing him instantly.

Saber pushes past the body, Patrick following, and they climb the staircase leading to the third floor.

                                        CUT TO:

EXT. COMPOUND - STREET

The neighborhood, awakened by the crash and gunfire, stirs to life. Hakim and the SEALs notice LIGHTS flipping on.

And down the block, a group of several young men appear on a
roof.

                    SEAL
          (raising his weapon)
     This is Echo 05, I've got unknowns
     gathering on the Southwest Rooftops.
     Hakim, move those guys back.

                    HAKIM
          (speaking in Pashto)
     Go back brothers, this is official
     government business, and there is
     nothing to see here!!

                    SEAL
     I'm going to start wasting them.

                    HAKIM
     Please! They will kill you!

The onlookers pause. SEAL aiming lasers dance across their
chests.

                    HAKIM (CONT'D)
     They will kill you!

They turn and go.

INT. MAIN HOUSE - SECOND FLOOR - HALLWAY

- SEALs clear the SECOND floor as women and children flow
into the hallway... A SEAL grabs one of the wives and pulls
her out into the hallway, while another female disappears
behind a large REFRIGERATOR, and he grabs her too.

INT. MEDIA ROOM - SECOND FLOOR - CONTINUOUS

Justin opens a file cabinet, stuffed with documents.

INT. MAIN HOUSE SECOND TO THIRD FLOOR STAIRWAY

Saber is climbing the stairs, gun up, towards the third floor,
when he sees a flash of movement across the landing above
him. He stops climbing and -

                    SABER
          (calling out)
     Osama! Osama!?

Beat.

Beat.

Sweat on Saber's face

                    SABER (CONT'D)
     Osama!?

A man appears at the end of the third floor hallway.

-- Ssssht ! a bullet strikes him in the head - knocking him back into a bedroom

- Saber fires again, missing

- And proceeds down the hallway, going full speed now, Patrick right behind him, sprinting into the bedroom

INT. MAIN HOUSE OSAMA'S LIVING QUARTERS

Two women stand at the entrance of the room. Saber rushes them and with a football tackle, slams them into the wall.

Patrick enters the room and fires several rounds into the man on the floor.

                    PATRICK
               (into radio)
          Possible jackpot.

The women Saber is restraining are wailing, struggling to get to their husband, as a ten year-old boy rushes up to the body. Patrick pushes him away and kneels down to get a better look at the body.

                    PATRICK (CONT'D)
               (to Saber)
          Dude, do you realize what you just
          did?

                                        CUT TO:

INT. MAIN HOUSE - THIRD FLOOR ROOM - HALLWAY

JARED questions the wives.

                    JARED
               (in ARABIC)
          Who is he?

                    WOMAN
          He is al Noori Hasan.

                    JARED
               (shouting back to
                Patrick)
          She says it's not him.

                    PATRICK
          Talk to a kid.

Jared kneels down next to a nine year-old girl huddled in the corner and snaps open a chem light. He gives her the glowing green wand.

                    JARED
              (in Arabic)
         Daughter, what is his name?

The girl makes no reply.

                                        CUT TO:

INT. ASSAULT COMMAND CENTER - JALALABAD FORWARD OPERATING
BASE - EVENING

                    COMMANDING OFFICER   (O.S.)
              (through the radio)
         For God and Country, Geronimo.

Maya gasps.

EXT. DIEGO CORRIDOR - CONTINUOUS

The Commanding Officer issues orders.

                    COMMANDING OFFICER
              (into radio)
         All Stations: target secure, target
         secure.

INT. THIRD FLOOR - MASTER BEDROOM

                    PATRICK
              (into radio)
         Roger. Copy. Target Secure.

                    COMMANDING OFFICER   (O.S.)
         Target Secure - commence SSE.

INT. SECOND FLOOR - MEDIA ROOM

Justin flicks on the lights. Moving fast he picks up a
COMPUTER tower and throws it to the floor, cracking it open,
rips out the HARD DRIVE and tosses that into the bag.

As we pull back and realize the enormity of the task in front
of him -

The lights show an organized office, crammed with information,
stacks of files, disks, video equipment.

Twenty years of jihad.

                    JUSTIN
              (to his team)
         Do not leave a hard drive.

The SEALs gather everything they can.

INT. MAIN HOUSE - THIRD TO SECOND FLOOR STAIRWAY

Saber walks down the staircase in a daze. We stay with him
as he descends, noting the faraway look in his eyes -

INT. MAIN HOUSE - SECOND FLOOR - MEDIA ROOM

Saber walks into the office where the SSE (Sensitive Sight
Exploitation) is underway.

                    JUSTIN
               (to Saber)
          What's up?

                    SABER
          I shot the third floor guy.

                    JUSTIN
          Good for you. You want to help?

Justin tosses him an SSE bag.

                                             CUT TO:

INT. ASSAULT COMMAND CENTER - JALALABAD FORWARD OPERATING
BASE - EVENING

The command team studies their monitors.

                    PRINCE 52 PILOT O.S.
               (over radio)
          QRF inbound.

                                             CUT TO:

EXT. DIEGO CORRIDOR

The COMMANDING OFFICER is talking on two radios at once -
one to his men, the other to brass back at Jalalabad base.

                    COMMANDING OFFICER
               (into radio)
          Echo 05, this is Red 02, how long do
          you need for SSE?

INT. SECOND FLOOR - MEDIA ROOM

                    JUSTIN
               (into radio)
          At least ten minutes.

EXT. DIEGO CORRIDOR

                    COMMANDING OFFICER
               (into radio)
          You have four.

INT. SECOND FLOOR - MEDIA ROOM

                    JUSTIN
               (into radio)
          This is a gold mine, I need more
          time than that.

EXT. DIEGO CORRIDOR

                    COMMANDING OFFICER
               (into radio)
          If you're not at the LZ in four, I'm
          going to leave your ass behind.

INT. SECOND FLOOR - MEDIA ROOM

Justin yells to his team.

                    JUSTIN
          Four minutes!

                                             CUT TO:

EXT. HELO CRASH

Hakim arrives at the crashed helo. He crawls into the
interior and finds a BLACK BODY BAG. We follow this bag:

INT. MAIN HOUSE FIRST FLOOR

Hakim jogs into the main house with the BODY BAG, and through
his POV, we see slow down for the first time since the raid
began, noting the destruction:

- *blood stains on the walls,*

- *Bodies pierced with bullets,*

- *Wailing children.*

                    HAKIM
               (into coms)
          Where do you need the bag?

                    SEAL (O.S.)
          Third floor.

                                             CUT TO:

INT. THIRD FLOOR - MASTER BEDROOM

SEALs roll the body into the BAG as Patrick and another SEAL
collect articles of interest. Two SEALs zip up the bag and
carry it out. Just as...

INT. MEDIA ROOM - SECOND FLOOR

Justin's team leaves the office.

EXT. MAIN COURTYARD - A MOMENT LATER

The body bag is laid in the courtyard.

EXT. HELO CRASH - CONTINUOUS

The EOD SEAL slides into the belly of Prince 51. While he places charges, another SEAL climbs up to affix charges to the roof and rotors ...and like a tight roper, he walks out on the tail of the helicopter, when suddenly his foot slips, piercing the tail's thin skin, and he nearly falls off.

He manages to place a last charge - but the remainder of the tail piece will not be detonated.

EXT. COMPOUND - POTATO FIELD

Back at the whirling helicopter, the SEALs shove the BODY BAG into the interior compartment and jump in after it.

The helo rises into the night.

                                                    CUT TO:

EXT. HELO CRASH - CONTINUOUS

PRINCE 51 explodes, sending shrapnel and a fireball high into the air

EXT./INT PRINCE 52 - CONTINUOUS

The SEALs watch the flames as the compound shrinks beneath them

EXT. COMPOUND - ANIMAL PEN - CONTINUOUS

The fire of the exploded crashed helo blazes in the night.

INT. PRINCE 52 - A MOMENT LATER

The SEALs sit silent in the cabin, body bag at their feet.

                                                    CUT TO:

EXT. LANDING ZONE - JALALABAD FORWARD OPERATING BASE - LATER

Bathed in the bright white lights, Maya waits for the helo.

Concern on her face.

At last, she hears it.

A moment later, PRINCE 52 hovers into view and lands. Patrick and several SEALs run out, carrying the bag...

INT. HANGAR

The place is swarming with SOLDIERS, SEALs, and FBI agents with large bio-metric scanners - loud shouting everywhere: "mark media, first floor, who has a pen, etc."

EXT. LANDING ZONE

Maya makes her way towards the hangar tent.

INT. HANGAR

She pushes through the busy SEALs.

Maya sees it now - way in the corner of the hangar.

She walks and walks towards the bag.

She is alone with it now.

She unzips the BAG

CU: Maya.

Seven years telescoping to this moment. The end of a journey.

She stares at the body for a moment then turns to look across
the room where ADMIRAL MCRAVEN meets her eye.

She nods.

                    ADMIRAL MCRAVEN
                  (into phone)
          Sir, the agency expert gave a visual
          confirmation. Yes, Sir, the girl.
          Hundred percent.

Maya gazes at the bloodied face, then turns away and zips
the bag...and leaves the tent.

Her eyes afire.

                                        CUT TO:

EXT. JALALABAD AIRSTRIP - EARLY DAWN

Maya waits on the tarmac, alone.

A C-17, one of the largest most impressive planes in the
American fleet, rolls to a stop and the hatch opens.

She climbs the ladder -

INT. C-17 - CONTINUOUS

The cavernous cargo plane is empty of passengers. The pilot
motions to the seats.

                    PILOT
          Are you Maya?

                    MAYA
          Yeah.

                    PILOT
          That's the only name they gave me.
                  (odd)
          You can sit wherever you want, you're
          the only one on the manifest.

Maya sits down, buckles in. The PILOT heads back to the
cabin

>   PILOT (CONT'D)
>   You must be pretty important, you
>   got the whole plane to yourself!

Beat.

>   PILOT (CONT'D)
>   Where do you want to go?

She's speechless.

Overwhelmed.

Finally, she lets go.

Those luminous eyes become pools of relief and pain.

CUT TO: BLACK

Q & A

WITH MARK BOAL
BY ROB FELD

You started as a journalist—

Mark Boal: I started out in newspapers, went on to narrative nonfiction magazine articles in the late '90s, and then began trying my hand at screenwriting.

Was that after the "Death and Dishonor" piece in **Playboy,** *which inspired* **In the Valley of Elah,** *or were you screenwriting before?*

MB: Actually, in 2002, Kathryn Bigelow optioned a piece I did called "Jailbait." It became a short-lived TV show on Fox that she directed. That was really my introduction to television and film. Then I continued on the dual track I'm on now, trying to merge the two disciplines. That really started with *The Hurt Locker,* which was based on reporting, and continued with *Zero Dark Thirty.*

How was working with Paul Haggis on **In the Valley of Elah** *as an intro to screenwriting? Did you learn much from him?*

MB: Sure. I worked with Paul on the story, and after that started developing *The Hurt Locker* with Kathryn. I learned a lot from him, which I thought would be transferrable to other projects, but which turned out to be specific to that movie. And that was the revelation: you start at the bottom of the hill every time.

Rob Feld is a screenwriter whose writings on film and interviews with noted filmmakers appear regularly in such publications as the Writers and Directors Guild journals, *Written By* and *DGA Quarterly*, as well as in the Newmarket Press Shooting Script® series.

What had you thought might be transferrable?

MB: *In the Valley of Elah* was a detective procedural. So I learned a lot from Paul about how those kinds of films can be structured. *The Hurt Locker* had a completely different structure that was episodic and much more like an anti-narrative. It was just a different ball game entirely.

And a different ball game on **Zero Dark Thirty,** *too?*

MB: Yes, because this was a ten-year historical epic, with 120 characters. It's also a procedural, but with this grand sweep that was unique for me.

How do you think about the screenplay as a document? I was reading **The Hurt Locker** *screenplay today. You're a visual writer in your journalism, but also you're highly specific as to what we're seeing and when, really blocking it out on the script page.*

MB: I learned to write from my editors and that's sort of the imagistic style of New Journalism. They used to say, "Sights and sounds." Kathryn showed me what the demands of a screenplay were for a director: it's writing designed to be performed.

Can you describe some of those specific screenplay demands?

MB: A greater reliance on dialogue. The prose is less pivotal. There are some similarities; writing on some level is writing, and storytelling is storytelling. But there's a huge amount of compression that goes on in a film, so I had to learn as a screenwriter to be concise and careful with imagery because each individual image is so large and powerful on a movie screen.

Do you think about making it a pleasant read as well?

MB: Yes. I hope it's a pleasure to read, or people won't read it. And hopefully you can convey some of the emotion that you would like to see in the film in the screenplay.

Zero Dark Thirty *led a number of lives over the course of five years before it came to its final incarnation. Can you tell me something about that?*

MB: It started out as a whole different project about the failed effort to kill Osama bin Laden in Tora Bora in 2001 in Afghanistan. I worked on that movie for a couple of years, researching and writing, and we were just about to film when out of the blue bin Laden was killed. I decided to throw that script out and start again.

And what was that first approach about thematically?

MB: Thematically that was about two worlds colliding. American forces trying to work with local Afghan forces; this culture clash between, say, Detroit and Kabul.

Was that inspired by some frustration you heard expressed by soldiers?

MB: Yeah. That was also based on firsthand accounts of Delta operators I got to know who were on the ground in Tora Bora. It was a surreal situation for them to be given a backpack full of cash, dropped into a foreign country, and told, "Okay, go start a war and go kill this guy who lives up in the mountains." And it's not like they didn't try, it's just that it was a remarkable adventure, and to me indicative of the tunnel vision of U.S. military thinking at the time.

Military thinking or overall governmental strategy?

MB: I guess both. I guess it was political too.

So you had the Tora Bora version—

MB: We were pretty close to filming it. We had cast, Kathryn was ready to direct it, we were scouting and then turned on the TV one day and Osama bin Laden had been killed. At this point I was sort of married to the subject, so I either walk away and never think about bin Laden ever again, or throw that material out and start over. I asked Kathryn what to do, and she said start again. Since I usually listen to her, I started again.

Research as well?

MB: Pretty much. Some of the contacts were helpful, and having been familiar with the space, I knew which stop on the Metro to get off at to go to the Pentagon. But it was starting all over in terms of the creative process.

Tell me about the research. Obviously you spoke to a lot of people who were involved.

MB: Spoke to a lot of people, knocked on a lot of doors, spent a couple of months doing the old-fashioned reporting of calling everybody I knew, talking to as many people as I could. And I was fortunate to be able to speak with a lot of the people who had firsthand knowledge of the events, and craft characters based on the real people that were involved.

I'm amazed people were willing to talk to you.

MB: For the most part they were because they knew that in a movie their work could be portrayed without their identities being compromised.

So you really didn't know what the story was going to be when you set out?

MB: Nope. I was finding the story as I was reporting it. And the story changed a few times in the course of the reporting.

Characters as well?

MB: The characters changed based on who I talked to.

How would you characterize your accounting as history?

MB: I think there's going to be a lot of books written about this, and a lot of articles. I hope we're consistent with that material. I hope that it stands the test of time so that five or ten years from now, people can look back on it and say, "That's not a bad first draft." I double-checked sources and fact-checked the entire piece. I hope that the script tracks closely with actual events, although some alterations of dialogue and character occurred in the act of dramatizing and compressing ten years into two-and-a-half hours, and quite a bit had to be done to protect the identities of those depicted. But that was that, really. We shot the first draft.

This is more of an observation than a question, but I think it bares noting that the lead character is female, which is rare in stories such as this.

MB: Yes. Well, that really took me by surprise. I mean, I wasn't aware of the prominence of women at the CIA.

One of the things that I found so compelling and successful with the film was that you stayed character-based. It's highly informational, and there's certainly a lot of action—movement, locations, things to keep track of—but you really are rooted strongly in the characters and their subtleties.

MB: I love character studies, so to me the whole point of doing this is to look at the people involved. The information is the water that they swim in, but the subject matter is the people, the commitment that borders on fanaticism, and at the end of the day, they're quite interesting, right? They're heroic but fallible. They make mistakes, they suffer, they inflict pain on others. They're human. So I guess as it turns out, even in the ruthless calculus of the war on terror, there are still human individuals brimming with weird, irreducible particulars that have yet to be homogenized by the systems of power and control. As it turns out, those human traits survived even in the darkest of undisclosed locations. I guess I find that encouraging. And you know, if I was going to be slightly less didactic about it too, Jennifer Ehle plays a CIA officer who says, "To big breaks and the little people that make them happen." I like that sentiment in that line.

You tell us so little about her that I was surprised by how satisfying I found the story of her character.

MB: I tend to think that backstory sometimes gets in the way of identification with the character. So there was the choice to let her be as existentially defined by what you see, and not try to explain it. How can you ever explain human motivation anyway? So at a certain point you just say, "You know what? Let's just assert that this human being exists and she operates in this way, and hopefully that's dramatic."

Can you say more about that feeling, that backstory gets in the way?

MB: When I meet somebody, I really don't care what they did when they were six. I am not like a big Freudian. I just want to know what they're saying right now. So for me it gets in the way. And to me, if the motivation doesn't seem natural in the scene, then maybe the scene isn't that well constructed. Also, to create something that feels voyeuristic, backstory in some way fights that by imposing an authorial or even omniscient point of view, which is the opposite of what I'm trying to achieve.

And you're working in an aesthetic that feels immediate.

MB: It's meant to be visceral and as granular as possible. It's not the ten-thousand-foot view that interests me. It's the ten-foot view. Or at least, I should say that if I try to look at the big picture, I want to be looking up at it from ten feet rather than down from on high.

You do get into more backstory in your journalism. I wonder if you are seeing an evolution in your writing as a result?

MB: No, I just think that reporting is better suited to the ten-thousand-foot view. That's where you can go high up. Films to me are made of people, not policy, you know? You are photographing an individual, not a branch of sociology. Films are made with close-ups and medium shots. So that to me dictates what the writing should be like.

You also show a Muslim CIA officer praying, rolling up his carpet, and then continuing with the business of catching bin Laden. And you never comment upon it.

MB: It was something I discovered in the reporting. It's so implausible and yet makes perfect sense. This is how seriously they take their jobs; this is truly the variety of religious experience. But why comment on it, beyond the comment of including it?

While you had known actors, you and Kathryn made the film quite deliberately without movie stars, although you could have gotten any number of people to do it. I imagine that was a creative choice.

MB: That's really a directing choice that Kathryn has articulated, that she wants to instill the illusion of naturalism and authenticity. And part of that is casting people who don't come to the screen with such a big public persona, which eclipses what the character is trying to do.

Can you tell me about the choice of Jessica Chastain for the role of Maya?

MB: Kathryn wanted her for a long time but Jessica was unavailable, then after Jessica read the script she dropped out of another project to do ours. The typical Hollywood shuffle. Turned out to be a terrific choice I think.

You had an incredible amount of information to pepper throughout your story. How did you approach keeping it dramatic?

MB: Mind-numbing. It was a mind-numbing amount of information. Just an avalanche, and massively unpleasant to try to figure out all that stuff. The only way to dramatize it is to tell it through the eyes of the people for whom that information was important. Unless you create characters that are identifiable, you've got a real problem because the information is dense, exotic, and sort of impenetrable on a lot of levels.

How did you approach the structure? Did you literally outline, or did you jump right in?

MB: I didn't outline per se on this one. But I had a lot of notes. You look at ten years and try and pick what are the hundred or so most important events, and what are the key turning points in the story.

I saw you discuss somewhere how your journalistic experience influenced the dialogue that you write; how there's a necessity to remember exactly what people said. Was that something you brought with you to **Zero Dark Thirty?**

MB: I don't know if that's true anymore. I think that was true for a while, but I think I'm writing dialogue that's a little different now.

How so?

MB: I hope it's still naturalistic, but I'm feeling more comfortable in adding spin on the ball in terms of theatricality, using zingers and so forth. The dialogue in *The Hurt Locker* was rigorously un-theatrical by comparison. That said, you are right about the influence of journalism. *Zero Dark Thirty* is still drawn from life; if not always word for word, I still try to be faithful to the spirit of the group of people that I'm depicting. CIA officers, often chosen for language and analytical skills, tend to be highly verbal and articulate.

Those audio recordings from 9/11; were you always going to begin the film with them?

MB: Always. Even in the Tora Bora script. I felt that the imagery had grown into something else; with the repetition, I couldn't bear to see those images again. But there was something about the voices that felt appropriate.

Which seemed to give you enough to go the whole movie without showing the bad guy.

MB: Well, that's because I didn't interview him. Peter Bergen is the only guy I know of who has interviewed him.

So, given a strictly fictional piece—

MB: I would drown. I need to start with reporting.

Still, though, you resisted showing even a flash of bin Laden, to instill in the audience—

MB: My characters never got to meet him so it would break the narrative rules of the script to cheat that. I hope he exists as a specter; he haunts their lives every day. I tried to make him a felt presence without making him somebody you saw on screen.

And yet maintain the suspense his ongoing existence demands.

MB: Yes, his reign didn't really end with 9/11. There was a series of attacks that continued for the next decade, and for the people within the intelligence world, those attacks were devastating. You know, it's a global war, but like all wars it's very personal. It's very much you hit us, we hit you. The Cold War was like that too.

Knowing you would finance this film independently and make it without support from the military, did that affect the scripting?
MB: It didn't really affect the script.

But it was going to affect access you had to locations and military equipment.
MB: Totally. Not working with governments means that it's harder to get military equipment. But, you know, computer graphics is a lot cheaper these days. So in the old days, if you were making a military movie and you needed a helicopter, you had absolutely no choice but to go to the U.S. government and submit your script for approval. These days you can rent a helicopter from the Jordanian military. If the helicopter doesn't look the way you want it to, you can hire a computer graphics company in Toronto. There's a lot that the computer revolution has done to give filmmakers independence.

Straddling both worlds of film and journalism, is there a general way you've seen your screenwriting head affect your journalistic writing?
MB: Not really. To me reporting is like going to church; nobody cares who you are or what meetings you can get in Hollywood. For some crazy reason I like that. But screenwriting has unique pleasures as well. It's all well and good to write a character, but when you see that character being performed by a Mark Strong or a Stephen Dillane, and you think, "Wow, they've just taken these words and animated them in a way that is far beyond what I could have imagined." And I think that's the gift of a performing art; your work gets to live through other people, which is an amazing thing that a prose writer doesn't experience.

As an apparent result of the research you do, it strikes me that the worlds you paint are laden with authority. Do you demand a certain level of command over material before you get into it?

MB: I like to know as much as I can. That gives me the confidence to write about it. I'm not very confident in my own guesswork.

You're obsessive with detail, which is part of what gives reality to so much of what you do.

MB: I find detail comforting, so I tend to build everything out of a lot of it. To me it's like the little breadcrumbs along the way. I wish I could let go if it sometimes, and that was also true of my journalism; it would just be a spray of details. It's not something I'm super-proud of in my work, but it is what it is. I'm a detail freak.

I think it paints the world and makes it distinctive.

MB: It can also be overwhelming. And that's where a good editor comes in handy.

You're highly involved in many aspects of production, not just the script. You produced on both **Zero Dark Thirty** *and* **The Hurt Locker.**

MB: I like producing because it's social and you get to be in the mix with all these really interesting, creative people. To be honest, it's a lot more fun than writing. And the pay off is tremendous, creatively, which is something that might sound counterintuitive. And you know, Kathryn taught me a long time ago, if you want to get a movie made you better make it yourself.

Most screenwriters aren't allowed this close to production and to post-production.

MB: I think more screenwriters should become producers. They're ostensibly the guardians of the story. But also, by the way, Kathryn and I have a unique working relationship that I don't think I could replicate. So it's really not about being about a producer per se. It's more that I happen to have formed a partnership with a brilliant director who tolerates having me around.

The idea of the unsung heroes seems to move you.

MB: For me, it's not really about heroism, or at least not consciously. It is looking at the big event refracted through the person that you least expect. And it's using this humanity to make the larger points. The trope goes back to Dickens, and I grew up with it in magazines. I'm a sucker for the little guy. Whether they're heroic or not, that's beside the point.

What you've written in film thus far deals greatly with what the experience of fighting a war does to the people who have to go fight it. **In the Valley of Elah,** *certainly* **The Hurt Locker—**

MB: Warriors, yes.

Warriors. You were very close to those experiences as an embedded journalist. I'm wondering what being so close to it did even to you?

MB: Part of it is you don't really pick the story, the story picks you. I wasn't particularly interested in the military until 9/11, and then that day hit me on a personal note because I was born in New York, and the personal resonance led to a professional focus. I'm attracted and repelled by these people so it seems like fertile ground, but beyond that I don't really know. I could invent a motivation for you but it would just be me giving you an idea that sounds elegant, or logical. What writer ever really knows why they pick this or that? It just seems to be where I've ended up.

STORYBOARDS

16

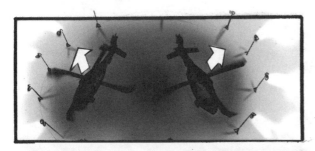

HIGH AS THE BLACKHAWKS
RISE . .

17

MIA WATCHES

18.1

PAST MIA AS THEY RISE
AND THE WE PAN

18.2

... AS THEY PASS OVER-
HEAD...

18.3

... AND AWAY, TOWARD
THE TARGET ,

p.4

2.35:1 GARY THOMAS 2011

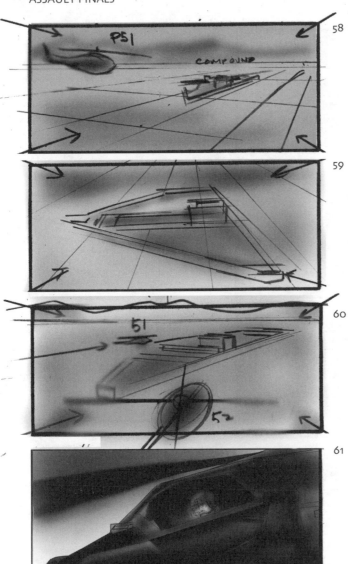

58

59

60

61

62

P.O.V. FROM PRINCE 52 AT 51 NEARING THE COMPOUND.

CONTINUED P.O.V. AS THEY DESCEND TO THE LANDING SITE.

FOLLOWING 52 W/51 DROPPING DOWN IN B.G.

UP AT PILOT.

P.51 P.O.V. OF APPROACHING COMPOUND

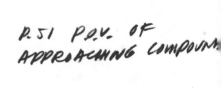

2.35:1 GARY THOMAS

63

HE FEATHERS THE CONTROLS.

64.1

DROP DOWN AS
P.52 STARTS TO
ROCK. P.52 LANDS
IN THE B.G.

64.2

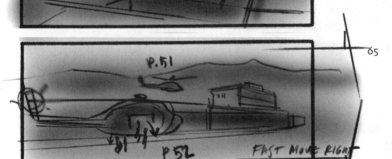

P.51 STARTS
TO ROCK AS
P.52 LANDS

65

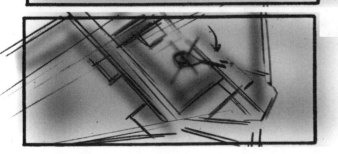

AT. P.52 AS
5 TROOPS JUMPS
OUT.

66

HIGH DRONE P.O.V.
OF P.51 GOING
INTO UNSTABLE
ROTATION.

2.35:1 GARY THOMAS 2011

67

DUST CURTAINS RISE
VERTICALLY AS THE WALLS
FORCE THE WINDFLOW
UPWARD.

68

THE TAIL SECTION
NARROWLY MISSES
THE ROOF OF THE
GUEST HOUSE.

69

LOW/UP AS THE TAIL
PASSES OVER THE WALL.

70

THE TAIL SHIFTS RAPIDL

71

THE PILOT CONCENTRATES.

P.16

2.35:1 GARY THOMAS

72

THE WHOLE CRAFT SHUTTER VIOLENTLY AS THE LIFT FAILS.

73

HE USES ALL HIS SKILL TO FIGHT THE CONDITIONS.

74

INTERIOR AS DUST FILLS THE CABIN.

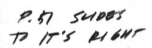

75.1.

P. 51 SLIDES TO IT'S RIGHT

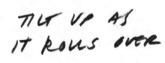

75.2

TILT UP AS IT ROLLS OVER

p.17

119

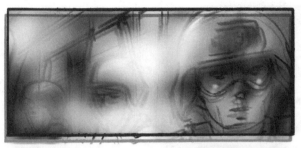

76

PATRICK SEES...

77

...THE ANIMALS SCATTER AS THEY COME DOWN HARD.

78

THE CHOPPER IS UNSTABLE AND ROCKS TO THE LEFT.

79

PATRICK NEARLY FALLS OUT BUT HIS BUDDY GRABS HIS ARM.

80

PATRICK SMILES - THANKS.

p.18

81

AT PILOTS AS THEY BATTLE
THE TURBULENCE.

82

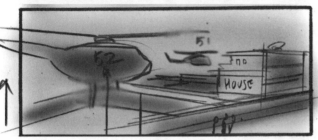

LIFT UP w/ P.52
P.51 IN B.G.

83.1

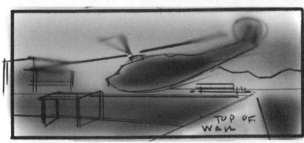

FROM TOP OF
WALL AS P.51
LOSES ALTITUDE...

83.2

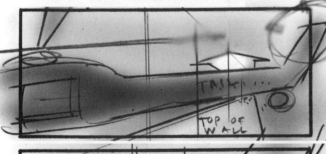

FROM THE TOP OF THE
WALL AS THE TAIL
SLIDES ALONG THE
SURFACE.

83.3

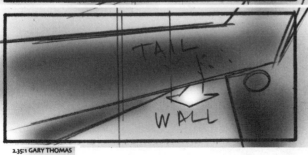

...CONTINUED...
IT RIPS THROUGH
THE BARBED WIRE.

2.35:1 GARY THOMAS

p.19

84.1

UP AT BLACKHAWK AS
THE NOSE PITCHES FORWARD.

84.2

... AND DIVES INTO THE
SOFT DIRT.

85.1

HIGH / OVERHEAD P.O.V. OF
FIRST CHOPPER AS IT
LANDS. THE TAIL SECTION
CRASHING DOWN ON THE
HIGH WALL.

85.2

A DUST CLOUD OBLITERATE
VISIBILITY.

86

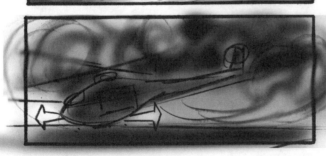

... LOW / GROUND
LEVEL AS THE
NOSE SCRAPES

p.20

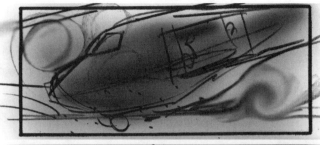

87

IT SLIDES
RIGHT UP
TO CAMERA.

88

THE P.O.V. OF P.51
FROM P.52

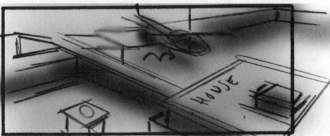

89

DRONE P.O.V. AS THE
SECOND BLACKHAWK
MOVES TOWARD THE ROOF.

90

UP AT PILOT.

2.35:1 GARY THOMAS

91

2ND B.H. P.O.V. OF
PILOT.

p.21

92

LOW/UP AT PRINCE
52 AS IT DESCENDS.
DEBRIS IS THROWN
FROM THE ROOF...

93

INSIDE, THE SEALS ARE JOLTED
BUT QUICKLY MOVE TO EXIT.

94

PATRICK LEADS THE MEN
AS THEY LEAP FROM THE
OPEN DOOR.

95

PAST PATRICK AS HE
LANDS. THE COMPOUND
VISIBLE IN THE B.G.

96

AS THEY RUN,
THE SEALS DUCK TO
AVOID GETTING
HIT BY THE STILL-
ROTATING MAIN BLADES.

p.22

97.1

LOW/ UP AT PRINCE
52 AS IT DESCENDS.
DEBRIS IS THROWN
FROM THE ROOF...

97.2

TILT TO

(TILT DOWN TO...)

...SEALS ADVANCE
AS THINGS DROP
IN FRONT OF THEM.

98

LOW/ AT SEALS, AS
A SAT DISH CRASHES
DOWN.

99

PRINCE 52 ABANDONS
THE DROP AND FLIES
AWAY.

100

SEALS MOVE TO
THE GATE.

P.23

2.35:1 GARY THOMAS

CAST AND CREW CREDITS

COLUMBIA PICTURES PRESENTS

AN ANNAPURNA PRODUCTION A FIRST LIGHT PRODUCTION A MARK BOAL PRODUCTION
A KATHRYN BIGELOW FILM

"ZERO DARK THIRTY"

JESSICA CHASTAIN JASON CLARKE JOEL EDGERTON

JENNIFER EHLE MARK STRONG KYLE CHANDLER EDGAR RAMIREZ and JAMES GANDOLFINI

CHRIS PRATT CALLAN MULVEY FARES FARES REDA KATEB HAROLD PERRINEAU STEPHEN DILLANE

Directed by KATHRYN BIGELOW	Executive Producers GREG SHAPIRO COLIN WILSON TED SCHIPPER	Costumes Designed by GEORGE L. LITTLE
Written by MARK BOAL		Music by ALEXANDRE DESPLAT
Produced by MARK BOAL KATHRYN BIGELOW MEGAN ELLISON	Director of Photography GREIG FRASER, ACS Production Designer JEREMY HINDLE	Sound Design PAUL N.J. OTTOSSON Casting MARK BENNETT CSA RICHARD HICKS CSA GAIL STEVENS
	Edited by DYLAN TICHENOR, A.C.E. WILLIAM GOLDENBERG, A.C.E.	

CAST (in order of appearance)

DAN	Jason Clarke
AMMAR	Reda Kateb
MAYA	Jessica Chastain
JOSEPH BRADLEY	Kyle Chandler
JESSICA	Jennifer Ehle
JACK	Harold Perrineau
THOMAS	Jeremy Strong
J.J.	J.J. Kandell
DETAINESS ON MONITOR	Wahab Sheikh
	Alexander Karim
	Nabil Elouahabi
	Aymen Hamdouchi
	Simon Abkarian
INTERROGATORS ON MONITOR	
	Ali Marhyar
	Parker Sawyers
	Akin Gazi
	Derek Siow
HAKIM	Fares Fares
CARGO SHIP DETAINEE	Mohammad K
BAGRAM GUARD	Henry Garrett
HASSAN GHUL	Homayoun Ershadi
PAKISTANI DETENTION CENTER GUARD	
	Darshan Aulakh
FARAJ COURIER	Navdeep Singh
ABU FARAJ AL-LIBBI	Yoav Levi
PAKISTANI GUARD AT MARRIOTT	
	Sukhdeep Singh
HUMAM KHALIL AL-BALAWI	Musa Sattari
CASE OFFICER	David Menkin
JOHN	Scott Adkins
ZIED	Eyad Zoubi
BLACKWATER GUARD	Julian Lewis Jones
C.I.A. SECURITY	Christian Contreras
LAUREN	Lauren Shaw
EMBASSY TECH	Zachary Becker
GEORGE	Mark Strong
ANALYST AT EMBASSY	John Antonini
DEBBIE	Jessica Collins
THE WOLF	Fredric Lehne
KUWAITI BUSINESSMAN	Ashraf Telfah
LARRY FROM GROUND BRANCH	
	Edgar Ramirez
TECH FROM GROUND BRANCH	
	Jonathan Olley
N.S.A. TECH	Ben Lambert
RAWAL CALLER	Manraaj Singh
ABU AHMED	Tushaar Mehra
TIM - STATION CHIEF	Daniel Lapaine
GUARD AT MAYA'S APARTMENT	
	Udayan Baijal
STEVE	Mark Duplass
C.I.A. DIRECTOR	James Gandolfini

NATIONAL SECURITY ADVISOR
. . . . Stephen Dillane
DEPUTY NATIONAL SECURITY ADVISOR
. . . . John Schwab
ASSISTANT TO NATIONAL SECURITY
ADVISOR . . . . Martin Delaney
PAKISTANI DOCTOR . . . . Nabil Koni
GENERAL IN HANGAR . . . . Anthony Edridge
JEREMY . . . . John Barrowman
DEPUTY DIRECTOR OF C.I.A. . . . . Jeff Mash
PATRICK - SQUADRON TEAM LEADER
. . . . Joel Edgerton
JUSTIN - DEVGRU. . . . . Chris Pratt
JARED - DEVGRU . . . . Taylor Kinney
SABER - DEVGRU . . . . Callan Mulvey
HENRY - DEVGRU . . . . Siaosi Fonua
PHIL - DEVGRU. . . . . Phil Somerville
NATE - DEVGRU EOD . . . . . . Nash Edgerton
MIKE - DEVGRU . . . . Mike Colter
SQUADRON COMMANDING OFFICER
. . . . Frank Grillo
DEVGRU OPERATORS. . . . . Brett Praed
Aron Eastwood
Heemi Browstow
Chris Scarf
Barrie Rice
Rob Young
Spencer Coursen
Chris Perry
Alex Corbet Burcher
Robert G. Eastman
Tim Martin
Mitchell Hall
P.T.
PILOTS . . . . Alan Pietruszewski
Kevin La Rosa II
Michael David Selig
Ben Parillo
ADMIRAL BILL MCCRAVEN
. . . . Christopher Stanley
ABU AHMED'S WIFE . . . . Hadeel Shqair
ABRAR . . . . Noureddine Hajjoujou
ABRAR'S WIFE . . . . Nour Alkawaja
UBL WIVES . . . . Malika Sayed
Rida Siham
Moula Mounia
Zalfa Seurat
KHALID . . . . Tarik Haddouch
OBL. . . . . Ricky Sekhon
C-130 PILOT. . . . . Mark Valley

STUNTS

STUNT COORDINATOR. . . . . . Stuart Thorp
ASSISTANT STUNT COORDINATOR
. . . . Rob Young

STUNT RIGGER . . . . Jason Oettle
STUNT PERFORMERS. . . . . . . Lauren Shaw,
Joseph Beddelem, Mustapha Touki, Othman Ilyassa,
Gaelle Cohen, Todor Petrov Lazarov, Elitsa
Razheva, Roza Dimitrova, Marina Jordanova,
Radka Snimki, Svetoslav Rangelov, Emil Tonev

CREW

UNIT PRODUCTION MANAGER
. . . . Colin Wilson
FIRST ASSISTANT DIRECTOR
. . . . David A. Ticotin

SECOND ASSISTANT DIRECTORS
. . . . Ben Lanning
Sarah Hood
CO-PRODUCERS . . . . Jonathan Leven
Matthew Budman
ASSOCIATE PRODUCER . . . . David A. Ticotin
KEY MAKE-UP AND HAIR DESIGN
. . . . Daniel Parker

SUPERVISING ART DIRECTOR
. . . . Roderick McLean
ART DIRECTOR . . . . Ben Collins
SET DECORATOR . . . . Lisa Chugg
SECOND UNIT DIRECTOR. . . John Mahaffie
SECOND UNIT DIRECTOR OF
PHOTOGRAPHY . . . . Simon Tindall
ADDITIONAL PHOTOGRAPHY
. . . . Ryley Brown
Duraid Munajim
FIRST ASSISTANT CAMERA . . . John Watters
Jake Marcuson
Henry Landgrebe
Tom Wilkinson
SECOND ASSISTANT CAMERA . . Beisan Elias
Paul Snell
SECOND UNIT FIRST ASSISTANT
DIRECTOR . . . . Udayan Baijal
SECOND UNIT SECOND ASSISTANT
DIRECTOR . . . . Ananya Rane
GAFFER . . . . Perry Evans
BEST BOY ELECTRICIAN . Richard Pattenden
ELECTRICIAN . . . . Mark Clark
KEY GRIP . . . . Kurt Kornemann
BEST BOY GRIP . . . . Jeff Bettis
DOLLY GRIP . . . . Ian J. Hanna
KEY MAKE-UP & HAIR ARTIST
. . . . Lesley Smith
MAKE-UP & HAIR ARTIST
. . . . Natasha Nikolic-Dunlop
ASSISTANT SET DECORATOR
. . . . Maudie Andrews

PRODUCTION BUYER . . . . Michael Standish
GRAPHIC ARTIST . . . . .Chris Kitisakkul
PROP MASTERS . . . . Warren Stickley
                                Roy Chapman
CHARGEHAND DRESSING . . . . Mitch Niclas
ON-SET PROPS . . . . Matthew Broderick
PROPS . . . . .Colin Ellis
SCRIPT SUPERVISOR . . . . Luca Kouimelis
SOUND MIXER . . . . Ray Beckett, C.A.S.
BOOM OPERATOR . . . . Peter Murphy
SPECIAL EFFECTS SUPERVISOR
. . . . Richard Stutsman
ASSISTANT COSTUME DESIGNER
. . . . .Dan Lester
COSTUMER SUPERVISOR . . . . . Darion Hing
KEY COSTUMER . . . . Tracey Millar
SET COSTUMERS . . . . Helene Belanger
                               Valerie Belegou
AGER/DYER . . . . Melanie Turcotte
UNIT PHOTOGRAPHY . . . . . .Jonathan Olley
DIGITAL IMAGING TECHNICIANS
. . . . Britt Cyrus
                               Eduardo Eguia
DIGILAB TECHNICIANS . . . . . . Robert May
                               Piers Leighton
TRANSPORTATION COORDINATOR
. . . . Steven Brigden
PRODUCTION CONTROLLER . Steev Beeson
FIRST ASSISTANT ACCOUNTANT
. . . . Ruba Kharuf
PAYROLL ACCOUNTANT . Brenda McClellan
COMPUTER PLAYBACK . . . . Compuhire
U.K. CASTING ASSOCIATES . Rebecca Farhall
                               Colin Jones
U.S. CASTING ASSOCIATE Charley Medigovich
ASSISTANT TO MS. BIGELOW . Brooke Nasser
LOCATION SECURITY . . . . Barrie Rice
JORDAN UNIT
PRODUCTION SUPERVISOR . Angela Quiles
PRODUCTION MANAGER
. . . . .Philippa Naughten
ART DIRECTOR . . . . Rhys Ifan
ASSISTANT ART DIRECTOR . . . . Samer Raie
SECOND ASSISTANT CAMERA . .David Bird
                               Tanya Marar
SECOND ASSISTANT DIRECTOR
. . . . Yanal Kassay
SECOND SECOND ASSISTANT DIRECTOR
. . . . Tarek Afifi
GAFFER . . . . Hosni Baqqa
ELECTRICIAN . . . . Jamie Mills
RIGGING GAFFER . . . . Ron Shane
PRACTICAL ELECTRICIANS . .Raymond Mills
                               Mohammad Isam

ELECTRICAL RIGGERS . . . . Iain Lowe
                               Paul Garratt
BEST BOY GRIPS. . . Mohammad Abu-Shawish
                               Firas Dehous
KEY RIGGING GRIP . . . . . . .Brian B. Malone
SOUND ASSISTANT. . . . . .Francisco Fernandez
ARMORER . . . . .David Fencl
ASSISTANT ARMORER . . . . Khalil Hareb
HAIRDRESSER . . . . Mahmoud Karajogly
MAKE-UP ARTIST . . . . Yelka Gutierrez
ASSISTANT MAKE-UP ARTIST. . Nada Al-Agha
PRODUCTION SECRETARY
. . . . Shereen Baddour
SECOND ASSISTANT ACCOUNTANT
. . . . Mohammad Al-Ahmad
CASTING . . . . Lara Atalla
SET COSTUMER . . . . . . .Setareh Samavi Ewazi
SEAMSTRESS . . . . Fikreyyeh Abu Khait
COSTUME ASSISTANTS . .Mohammad Mustafa
                               Nabil Khoury
CONSTRUCTION MANAGER . . Samy Keilani
ASSISTANT CONSTRUCTION MANAGER
. . . . .Samir Zaidan
CONSTRUCTION COORDINATOR
. . . . .Maye Nufal
SCENIC PAINTERS . . . . Brian Morris
                               Dean Dunham
PICTURE CAR COORDINATOR
. . . . .Fawaz Al-Zoubi
PICTURE CAR ASSISTANTS . .Garo Youmjian
                        Ali Mahmoud Al-Khlaelah
LOCATION MANAGER . . . . . Jamal Al Adwan
UNIT MANAGER . . . . .Gabaah Nawafleh
SPECIAL EFFECTS ON-SET
COORDINATOR . . . . Blair Foord
SPECIAL EFFECTS TECHNICIANS . Paul Vigil,
   Ernie Lanninger, Ernst Gschwind, Wolf Steiling
STEALTH HELICOPTER SPECIAL EFFECTS
SUPERVISOR . . . . .Neil Corbould
SPECIAL EFFECTS WORKSHOP
SUPERVISORS . . . . David Brighton
                               Stuart Heath
SENIOR TECHNICIANS . . . . . . .Kieran Reed,
   Timothy Stracey, Colin Umpelby, David Poole
UNIT PHOTOGRAPHY ASSISTANT
. . . . .Chris Linaker
FIRST ASSISTANT DIRECTOR
. . . . Scott Robertson
SECOND ASSISTANT DIRECTOR
. . . . Jonas Spaccarotelli
PROPERTY BUYERS . . . . Karim Kheir
                               Nasser Zoubi
SIGNWRITER . . . . Abdul Qader Miqdadi
TECHNICAL ADVISOR . . . . .Mitchell Hall

MILITARY LIAISON. . . . . Marwan Abbadi
TRANSPORTATION CAPTAIN . . Fadi Sweiss
CATERING CHEF . . . . Carlos Castillo
CATERING FURNISHED BY . . . .United Arab
                    For Tourism Investment Co.

INDIA UNIT
LINE PRODUCER . . . . Tabrez Noorani
ASSOCIATE PRODUCER . . . . . .Pravesh Sahni
UNIT PRODUCTION MANAGER
. . . . Rajeev Mehra
CASTING . . . . .Seher Latif CSA
ART DIRECTOR . . . . Dilip More
PROP MASTER . . . . Sunil Chhabra
PROPMAN . . . . Yogender Kumar
SET DECORATION BUYER. . Samudrika Arora
GRAPHICS . . . . .Gurubaksh Singh Raj
DIALECT COACH . . . . .Jerome Butler
PRODUCTION MANAGER . . . Kaushik Guha
MUMBAI COORDINATOR . . . .Rakesh Singh
DELHI COORDINATOR. . . . . . . Rahul Soni
LOCATION MANAGER . . . . . . .Rajesh Dham
BEST BOY GRIP . . . . Bidhan Chanda
GAFFER . . . . .Ramesh Sadrani
KEY MAKE-UP/HAIRDRESSER
. . . . Virginia Holmes
COSTUME SUPERVISOR . .Riyaz Ali Merchant
TRANSPORTATION CAPTAIN
. . . . .Bhawani Singh
TRAVEL COORDINATOR . . . Pradeep Arora
PICTURE VEHICLES. . . . . . . Trilok Nowlakha
CATERING HEAD . . . . .Rajiv Kampani
PRODUCTION SERVICES (INDIA)
PROVIDED BY . . . . India Take One Productions

UK UNIT
LOCATION MANAGER . . . . .Nick Fulton
UNIT MANAGER. . . . . .Charlie Simpson
PRODUCTION COORDINATOR
. . . . Harry Serjeant
ELECTRICAL BEST BOY. . . . . . David Sinfield
KEY GRIP . . . . .David Mcanulty
PROP MASTER . . . . .Muffin Green
CONSTRUCTION COORDINATOR
. . . . .Malcolm Roberts

SECOND UNIT
SECOND UNIT CAMERA OPERATOR
. . . . Simon Finney
                        Ben Wilson
SECOND UNIT FIRST ASSISTANT
CAMERA . . . . .Adam Coles
                        Chris Bain
SECOND UNIT SECOND ASSISTANT
CAMERA . . . . .Richard Jakes
                 Sebastian Barraclough
SECOND UNIT VIDEO ASSIST. . Gary Martinez

SECOND UNIT GAFFER. . . . . . . Mark Evans
SOUND MIXER . . . . Gary Dodkin
KEY MAKE-UP/HAIR ARTIST
. . . . .Renata Gilbert

AERIAL UNITS
AERIAL CAMERA OPERATORS - JORDAN
. . . . John Marzano
                        Adam Dale
GROUND AERIAL COORDINATOR -
JORDAN . . . . .Steve North
WESCAM TECHNICIAN - JORDAN
. . . . .David Francis
ECLIPSE TECHNICIAN - JORDAN
. . . . .Justin Webber
AERIAL COORDINATOR / CAMERA
PILOT - U.S. . . . . .Kevin La Rosa
AERIAL DIRECTOR OF PHOTOGRAPHY -
U.S.. . . . . David Nowell

POST PRODUCTION
FIRST ASSISTANT EDITORS . . Brett M. Reed
                     Chris Patterson
VISUAL EFFECTS EDITOR . . . . . . Harry Yoon
ASSISTANT EDITORS . . . . Patrick J. Smith
                     Brian G. Addie
                  Lara Khachooni
                   Banner Gwin
POST PRODUCTION ASSISTANT
. . . . Peter Dudgeon
VISUAL EFFECTS BY IMAGE ENGINE
VISUAL EFFECTS SUPERVISOR
. . . . .Chris Harvey
VISUAL EFFECTS PLATE SUPERVISOR. . . . .
                    Jeremy Hattingh
VISUAL EFFECTS PRODUCER
. . . . Geoff Anderson
VISUAL EFFECTS EXECUTIVE PRODUCER
. . . . Stephen Garrad
VISUAL EFFECTS COORDINATOR
. . . . .Victoria Mowlam
VISUAL EFFECTS ON SET MATCHMOVER
. . . . Stephen Chan
ASSET SUPERVISOR . . . . Barry Poon
MODELLERS . . . . .Moriba Duncan
                 Tomoka Matsumura
TEXTURE ARTISTS . . . . . . Muhammad Marri
                  Andy Martinez
RIGGERS . . . . Peter Rabel
LEAD MATCHMOVER . . . . Lee Alexander
ANIMATORS . . . . .Denny Bigras
                  Sebastian Weber
EFFECTS ARTISTS . . . . .Paul Faulkes
                  Andy Feery
                  Sam Hancock

LIGHTING/LOOK DEVELOPMENT LEAD
. . . . Matthias Lautour
LIGHTING ARTISTS . . . . . . Nicolas Chombart
Brian Burritt
Jason Gross
ROTO LEAD . . . . Jackie Mills
LEAD COMPOSITER. . . . . Jesus Lavin
COMPOSITE ARTISTS . . . . Reuben Barkataki,
Ian Plumb, Sigurjon Gardarsson, Eric Ponton
Jean-Francois Houde, Ricardo Quintero
Sam Johnston, Vicki Silva
Thijs Noij, Jayme Vandusen
Jim Parsons, Matt Yeoman
Chun-Ping, Gwen Zhang
MATTE PAINTERS . . . . Marco Iozzi
Kent Matheson
VISUAL EFFECTS BY ARCH 9 FILMS
COMPOSITING SUPERVISOR . . Jeremy Burns
COMPOSITOR. . . . . Craig Crawford
VISUAL EFFECTS BY XY & Z VISUAL
EFFECTS
VISUAL EFFECTS SUPERVISOR
. . . . Mike Uguccioni
COMPOSITORS. . . . . Jamie Baxter
Trinh Baxter
SOUND SUPERVISOR and SOUND DESIGN
. . . . Paul N.J. Ottosson
RE-RECORDING MIXER . . Paul N.J. Ottosson
SOUND EFFECTS EDITORS
. . . . Jamie Hardt, M.P.S.E.
Lee Gilmore
DIALOGUE EDITOR . . . . Robert Troy
ADR SUPERVISOR . . . . James Simcik
FOLEY EDITOR. . . . . Mark Pappas
FOLEY MIXER. . . . . John Sanacore, C.A.S.
FOLEY ARTIST. . . . . Alex Ulrich, M.P.S.E.
LOOP GROUP . . . . The Final Word
ASSISTANT SOUND EDITOR
. . . . Ryan B. Juggler, M.P.S.E.
SOUND INTERN. . . . . Donnie Saylor
RE-RECORDIST . . . . Fred W. Peck III
POST SOUND FACILITIES PROVIDED BY
SONY PICTURES STUDIOS, CULVER CITY,
CALIFORNIA
POST PRODUCTION ACCOUNTING
SERVICES . . . . Trevanna Post, Inc.
POST PRODUCTION ACCOUNTANT
. . . . Dee Schuka
ASSISTANT ACCOUNTANT . . . . . John Weber
MUSIC COMPOSED AND CONDUCTED BY
. . . . Alexandre Desplat
MUSIC PERFORMED BY . . . . . . The London
Symphony Orchestra
SOLO TRUMPET . . . . Phil Cobb

NEY. . . . . Kudsi Erguner
DUDUK . . . . Levon Minassian
ELECTRIC & ACOUSTIC CELLO
. . . . Vincent Segal
VIOLIN . . . . Dominique Lemonnier
RECORDED and MIXED by Sam Okell
ADDITIONAL RECORDINGS BY Alexandre
Firla at STUDIO ACOUSTI, PARIS
RECORDED at ABBEY ROAD STUDIOS,
LONDON
MIXED at STUDIO DE LA GRANDE ARMEE,
PARIS
SCORE PRODUCER . . . Dominique Lemonnier
SCORE MUSIC EDITOR. . . . . Gerard McCann
AURICLE OPERATOR . . . . Peter Clarke
SOUND ENGINEER . . . . Sam Okell
SCORE COORDINATOR. . . . . Xavier Forcioli
ORCHESTRATIONS . . . . . . Alexandre Desplat
Sylvain Morizet, Jean-Pascal Beintus,
Nicolas Charron
PROGRAMMING. . . . . Romain Allender
Dan Marocco
MUSIC PREPARATION. . Norbert Vergonjanne
Claude Romano
MUSIC EDITOR. . . . . Richard Ford
ADDITIONAL MUSIC EDITOR . . Oliver Hug
MUSIC SUPERVISOR . . . . John Bissell

"PAVLOV'S DOGS"
Written by Charles Maggio, Keith Huckins,
Andrew Gormley, Nick Forte and Chris Laucella
Performed by Rorschach
Courtesy of Gern Blandsten Records

"PYAAR HAI TUMSE"
Written by Amir Jamal, Nasir Hussain,
Nasir Ali Nasir
Performed by Amir Jamal
Courtesy of Kamlee Records Limited
By arrangement with The Orchard

"MOVE YA BODY"
Written by FULL FORCE, Lionel Bermingham,
Elijah Wells, Cordel Burrell, Natalie Albino, Nicole
Albino and Luis Diaz
Performed by Nina Sky featuring Jabba
Courtesy of Universal Records under license from
Universal Music Enterprises
Contains sample of "Coolie Dance Rhythm" by
Cordell "Scatta" Burrell
Courtesy of Greensleeves Records Ltd.
License arranged by Fine Gold Productions LLC

"NEED YOU NOW"
Written by Hillary Scott, Joshua Kear, Dave
Haywood and Charles Kelley
Performed by Lady Antebellum
Courtesy of Capitol Records Nashville
Under license from EMI Film & Television Music

"NIGHT SONG"
Written by Nusrat Fateh Ali Khan
Performed by Nusrat Fateh Ali Khan & Michael
Brook
Courtesy of Real World Records

"RISE UP" (featuring TOM MORELLO)
Written by Senen Reyes, Louise Freese, Demrick
Shelton Ferm, Thomas Morello
Performed by Cypress Hill feat. Tom Morello
Courtesy of Capitol Records, LLC
Under license from EMI Film & TV Music

"MURDER (2012)"
Written by Jimmy Gnecco
Performed by Ours
Courtesy of Miseryhead Music
By arrangement with Revolution Songs

DIGITAL INTERMEDIATE provided by
COMPANY 3
COLORIST . . . . .Stephen Nakamura
DIGITAL INTERMEDIATE PRODUCER
. . . . .Annie Johnson
DIGITAL CONFORM . . . . .Joe Ken
Paul Carlin
TITLE DESIGN . . . . BLT: AV, INC.
PUBLICIST . . . . The Angellotti Company
PRODUCTION LEGAL SERVICES
. . . . Irwin M. Rappaport, P.C.
PRODUCTION PLACEMENT
. . . . Stone Management, Inc.
PRODUCT PLACEMENT COORDINATORS
. . . . .Adam Stone
Cat Stone
SPECIAL THANKS
MINISTRY OF INFORMATION AND
BROADCASTING, GOVERNMENT OF
INDIA, ADMINISTRATION OF UNION
TERRITORY OF CHANDIGARH,
CHANDIGARH POLICE,
PEC UNIVERSITY OF TECHNOLOGY
CHANDIGARH (FORMERLY PUNJAB
ENGINEERING COLLEGE)
ROYAL FILM COMMISSION,
JORDAN
PINEWOOD SHEPPERTON STUDIOS

PRODUCERS ALSO WISH TO THANK
5.11, INC., APPLE, ATLANTIC SIGNAL,
CYALUME TECHNOLOGIES, DANIEL
WINKLER, DUCATI, GARMIN, GENERAL
DYNAMICS, INERT PRODUCTS, K9
STORM, LEATHERMAN TOOL GROUP,
LONDON BRIDGE TRADING COMPANY,
MODERN WARFARE, LLC, OPS-CORE,
SALOMON, SUUNTO, THALES
COMMUNICATIONS, VT MILTOPE,
WENDY ABNEY, ROEG SUTHERLAND,
BRYAN LOURD, BRIAN KEND, DARIN
FRIEDMAN, BRIAN SIBERELL, SALLY
WILLCOX, ALAN WERTHEIMER,
WARREN DERN, KEVIN HUVANE,
SPENCER COURSEN, BILL DUCHENE,
GLOVER PARK GROUP

AERIAL SERVICES provided by FLYING
PICTURES

GRIP AND ELECTRICAL EQUIPMENT
PROVIDED BY SLATE in JORDAN

ECLIPSE, CINEFLEX, and WESCAM CAMERA
SYSTEMS provided by PICTORVISION

PHOTOS PROVIDED BY GETTY IMAGES
VIDEO AND AUDIO CLIPS PROVIDED BY:
ITN SOURCE, AP ARCHIVE, T3MEDIA/CBS
NEWS, ABCNEWS VIDEOSOURCE, FOX
NEWS ARCHIVE, ITN SOURCE/REUTERS,
OUTPOST FILMS, NBC UNIVERSAL
ARCHIVES